THE PERFECT KISS

"You care nothing for love," Georgiana went on, well aware that she was no longer acting like the jovial, levelheaded Georgie he knew. But she didn't care. It didn't matter any more. "For you love isn't necessary when it comes to marriage. For you it is nothing but a business arrangement or something unpleasant that must be done."

"And for you?" His face was so close to hers that their noses nearly touched.

She tried to pull away from him. "Please get me out of here. I'm feeling extremely uncomfortable with all this . . . this closeness."

Somehow her attempt to move away had only brought her closer to him. They were standing now in what could only be called an embrace.

"You don't love him," he said softly. "You don't love him and you're not going to marry him."

"No."

"And you didn't kiss him."

"Of course not."

"You're going to kiss me." It wasn't a command or a request, it was only a statement.

For a moment she only stared at him, unable to comprehend the outrageousness of his presumption.

And then his lips touched hers. . . .

Books by Catherine Blair

THE SCANDALOUS MISS DELANEY

THE HERO RETURNS

ATHENA'S CONQUEST

A FAMILY FOR GILLIAN

A PERFECT MISMATCH

Published by Zebra Books

A PERFECT MISMATCH

Catherine Blair

ZEBRA BOOKS
Kensington Publishing Corp.
http://www.kensingtonbooks.com

ZEBRA BOOKS are published by

Kensington Publishing Corp.
850 Third Avenue
New York, NY 10022

All Kensington titles, imprints, and distributed lines are available at special quantity discounts for bulk purchases for sales promotion, premiums, fund-raising, educational or institutional use.

Special book excerpts or customized printings can also be created to fit specific needs. For details, write or phone the office of the Kensington Special Sales Manager: Kensington Publishing Corp., 850 Third Avenue, New York, NY 10022. Attn. Special Sales Department. Phone: 1-800-221-2647.

First Printing: March 2002
10 9 8 7 6 5 4 3 2 1

Printed in the United States of America

For Gabrielle Pantera, of the vast reference collection, infinite patience, and very valuable advice.

One

"He's perfect." Georgiana leaned her elbows on the railing of the narrow balcony that ringed the ballroom and looked down at the crowded assembly. "Absolutely perfect."

"Viscount Iverley? Perfect?" her mother exclaimed. "I would hardly go as far as that. Handsome I'll grant you." She examined the man through her lorgnette, then sighed. "One could hardly argue that he is well favored. But, my dear, everyone says he's wholly uninterested in society. He came to Lincolnshire solely for the hunting."

Mrs. Palmer put her lorgnette back into her reticule as though this entirely settled the question. "You would do better to set your sights on someone else, my dear. Perhaps Lord Pawson. Or even better, Lord Quigley. Though he is, perhaps, a bit too old for you. However, I never thought twenty years of any moment when I married your papa, rest his soul. Girls are a good deal too nice about age these days." She made a broad gesture that encompassed the room below them. "Really, there are any number of eligible, or nearly eligible, men up from London for the hunting season. I do wish you wouldn't be quite so particular."

Georgiana went back to watching Lord Iverley. She wasn't being particular. She had merely been waiting until she found the man Fate had meant her to be with. And now she'd found him. Her mother need no longer be anxious that, at the advanced age of twenty, she would end up on the shelf. She'd found him.

Iverley stood tall and broad-shouldered by the doorway to the card room. Though he was immaculately dressed in a dark coat and champagne-colored breeches, Georgiana knew from his reputation that he would have felt far more comfortable in a driving coat or riding boots. As her brother Richard said, Iverley was a top-o'-the trees Corinthian if there ever was one.

"Good heavens, here's Emily with her hair half down her back," her mother exclaimed as Georgiana's younger sister bounded up the stairs. "Come, let me fix it. If you would only dance with a little less vigor, my dear."

Emily rolled her eyes and submitted to her mother's ministrations. "Still up here mooning over that friend of Richard's?" she asked Georgiana. "Just our bad luck that the first handsome man to come to Lincolnshire would hate dancing."

"Just because he hasn't danced doesn't mean he hates dancing," Georgiana said mildly.

"There," said Mrs. Palmer, giving a hothouse rose one last twitch, "you're fairly presentable, anyway."

Emily kissed her mother on the cheek and then went to look over the balcony railing. "Everyone says that Lord Iverley has hardly come to a single party since he arrived. He sounds dreadfully dull." She leaned her chin on her fists and watched the swirling crowd below. "Mr. Hennings is down from London too, and *he* doesn't mind dancing. But he's covered with freckles. I suppose, however, that one could learn to overlook that. I would rather love a man with freckles than a dull dog who hates dancing."

Emily obviously had no idea of what made up perfection.

"Nonsense," Georgiana said with confidence. "Iverley is enjoying himself. I just saw him smile. Oh dear, it was merely a sneeze. But still, one could imagine what he would look like if he did smile." Just looking at him gave her a warm feeling of anticipation. He was here. In Lincolnshire. She'd thought it would be ages before she saw him again, but here he was. Fate indeed.

"Well, if he's a friend of Richard's, he likely cares for nothing but sporting and gambling. Corinthians," her sister continued with all the worldliness of her sixteen years, "do not make good beaux."

Georgiana made a noise of protest, but kept her eyes on the man in the room below. Iverley *was* perfect; anyone would think so. His dark hair shone a rich chestnut in the light of the chandeliers, and there was an athletic grace to his carriage. She'd met him only the one time, two weeks ago in London, but she wasn't likely to forget the strong lines of his face or the arresting paleness of his hazel eyes. He was the most handsome man in the room by far. And definitely the one with the most address in a provincial town assembly like this one.

Though, even in London he'd outshone them all. Her sister might think him dull for not dancing, but she had never had the good fortune to meet him. Emily was not destined for him. And she was.

"His father is the Earl of Eversham," her mother said suddenly, as though she had been mulling this over for a while. "Which counts for a good deal. But Quigley is a duke, which counts for a great deal more.

Besides, the earl is a young man, likely to live a score more years."

Destined. Georgiana would never forget the moment she discovered it. The day before they were to leave London for Lincolnshire, she'd been walking with Richard on Bond Street. It had been a day like any other. She was glad to be leaving London and was looking forward to spending the autumn quietly amusing herself with books and letters, when they had met Iverley coming out of a tailor's establishment. He'd said hello to her brother and then smiled and bowed over her hand while Richard made a rather offhanded introduction.

And the whole world had stopped.

Iverley's eyes looked down into hers, and for a moment she felt that there was no one in the world but the two of them, and that he had been waiting there on the corner all his life for her. She'd felt the inexplicable urge to throw herself into his arms and apologize for having kept him waiting.

Then he'd spoken with her brother for a moment and walked on as though nothing had happened. Still, a man couldn't very well make the world stop for you and not know that he'd done it. He must have felt it, too. A magic like that couldn't be made up in one's head.

She was glad now that she had turned down the two very respectable offers she had had during the Season and braved her mother's despair. Her mother needn't have worried. Now Iverley was here, for the whole glorious autumn, and everything would be just as it should be.

"Come, girls, you're not likely to meet Lord Perfect or anyone else when you're hiding up here. We must go down and see if Mr. Kirkland will make us introductions." Mrs. Palmer shooed them away from the balcony.

"He looks quite stern," Emily murmured as they followed their mother down the stairs. "And more than a little bored."

Georgiana frowned. "Of course he's bored. This is nothing compared to what he's used to."

"How do you know anything about him?" her sister demanded.

"I don't," she admitted. "But he just seems as though he is the kind of man who loves adventure. A man who has known great sadness and can feel great love."

Emily made a comical face of despair. "He's likely just dull-witted. So many of those sporting men are. Great sadness and love." She laughed. "You read too much poetry. If you spent more time dancing and less time daydreaming you'd have a great many more admirers." She shot her sister a look of mild censure. "You won't even *talk* to men."

Georgiana dismissed her sister's advice with a shrug. Talking to strangers made her uncomfortable, shy. But it was different with Iverley. He would understand her. The look in his eyes when she'd met him told her that he would understand her entirely.

"I don't know why you would prefer Lord Iverley to Mr. Hennings," her sister continued, pausing to wave with great enthusiasm to one of her friends across the room. Several blooms promptly fell out of her hair. *"He* has sent you posies at every excuse. And his father owns quite the largest house in the county."

"I don't love Hennings," Georgiana said simply. There could be no better reason than that.

She briefly caught sight of Lord Iverley through the crowd. He still stood leaning against the wall, his eyes half closed as he listened to young Tony Pawson tell an animated story to the group of men in the corner.

As she watched, Lord Hepswell, another of Richard's cronies, gave Iverley a nudge and pointed at a pretty girl in a yellow dress. She was standing by the doorway, looking conspicuously available for the next dance. Hepswell's bushy black brows waggled expressively, but Iverley shook his head and turned back to the conversation.

"And I know for a fact that Mr. McMahon has written you poetry every day since we left London," her sister continued doggedly. "Does he say your eyes are blue as cornflowers, like that dreadful Mr. Shawfield? I don't see why people can't think of anything but cornflowers. Frank Rowe said the same, didn't he? I hope when I'm out, my beaux will be able to think of better similes."

Iverley had shifted positions and was scowling into his glass of brandy. His friends were carrying on a spirited argument of some kind, but he seemed removed in his own thoughts. Something pulled strongly inside Georgiana at the look of sadness on his face.

"Now, my dear, whoever Mr. Kirkland introduces us to, do try to be a bit more vivacious," Mrs. Palmer said, turning back to her daughter. She took Georgiana's elbow and propelled her across the room. "Your greatest failing is that you're too retiring. Always with your nose in a book and your head in the clouds. If you would pay more attention to the world around you, you'd find that there are a great many young men who are quite interested in you." She sighed. "I do wish you hadn't turned off that nice man from Wales. I couldn't understand a word he said, but I hear he has seven thousand a year."

Mrs. Palmer caught the master of ceremoies' attention and gestured, then turned back to her daughter. "If you weren't so romantic, you wouldn't find yourself investing perfect strangers with every virtue. I imagine that if you knew this Lord Iverley better, you would find that he is nothing like what you've imagined him to be. If he's a friend of Richard's you'll have nothing in common with him. If you'd chosen a friend of your brother William, he would be ever so much more eligible. Will turned out a steady sort. I don't know where Richard gets his wild streak."

Georgiana smiled to herself. No, Iverley was nothing like Richard. True, he was one of the Corinthian crowd, dashing and athletic, ready for any lark, but why shouldn't that suit her? Just because she liked poetry and plays and couldn't always think of what to say to people, didn't mean she could not fall in love with a sporting man.

"You're not listening to a word I'm saying," her mother said correctly. "Very well, if you're so keen on him, why should we not find Richard and have him introduce you?"

Georgiana felt a stab of alarm. "What would I say?" She would never have the courage to actually talk to the man. For the moment, just knowing that Iverley was fated for her was enough. She had not actually considered actively pursuing him. Somehow, in her mind, he had been the one to come to her, admitting in his low, rich voice that he knew the moment he saw her that she was meant for him.

Mrs. Palmer, who had never suffered a moment's shyness in her life, looked at her daughter with some surprise. "Good heavens, my dear, there are a thousand ways to engage a man in conversation. Talk about things that interest him. Talk about the weather or the people here. Or better yet"—she tapped her fan on her chin—"ask his advice about something. Not an intellectual matter or anything personal, of course. You'll only alarm him and make him feel ignorant. Ask his advice on horseflesh or something about which you know he'll have an opinion."

She gave Georgiana an all-knowing smile and nodded vigorously. "You will never further yourself in his acquaintance if you do not make an effort to be pleasant in conversation. Your father said from the first that he admired my ability to discourse on any topic."

Georgiana, too, had often thought this talent remarkable.

"Your father, of course, preferred to talk about bird-watching," Mrs. Palmer continued. "I must admit that I found the topic quite incomprehensible at first, but I was always perfectly willing to talk about it. A woman must learn that even when she would really much rather talk about the perfectly sweet new bonnet she saw in the shop window on High Street, she should first let her husband talk about bird-watching. Men feel important if you show an interest in their projects."

Georgiana nodded obediently. As their entire house was papered with the drawings of birds Mama had made while bird-watching with Papa, she must assume that the woman had acquired some knowledge of the subject.

Iverley still wore that peculiar look of distraction. What Emily had mistaken for boredom looked to Georgiana like a certain wistfulness. She felt an instant desire to go to him, put her hand on his sleeve, and tell him that things would be all right now.

As she watched him, he gave his friends a tight smile, made an apologetic bow, and strode off toward the French doors leading out into the garden.

"Mama is right," Emily said, standing on tiptoe to scan the room. "You'll have to trot over there and put yourself under his nose. Remember, next Season is for me. We can each have only one, and it isn't my fault that you turned down every offer you had." She gave her sister an impish grin. "If you can't catch your Lord Perfect, I daresay we will have to marry you off to cousin Elliot."

Georgiana suppressed a shudder. Emily was only quizzing her, but she was more right than she knew. Only two days ago, her mother had given her a stern talking-to about her duty to the family and the folly of a young woman of no great fortune being too particular about her prospects of marriage.

Very well. Perhaps it was time to take Fate by the horns. Once Iverley saw her again, he would know, like she did, that they were destined to be together. She had the unexpected chance to see him for the whole of the hunting season, and she must make the most of it. For once in her life she knew what she wanted, and she would have it.

She opened her fan with a snap and straightened her shoulders. "You shall have your Season, Emily," she said regally. "And if you don't take, *you* can marry cousin Elliot. I"—she smiled with the quiet confidence of one who knew her future—"am going to marry Lord Iverley."

Two

Iverley cast a suspicious eye on the shrubbery. He'd toyed with the idea of a brisk walk there to get away from the crowds, but it now occurred to him that he was likely to interrupt more than one tryst in those darkened, leafy corners. He took a large swallow of brandy and set the empty glass into the open hand of a stone Cupid in the insipid act of blowing a kiss. A pack of mismatched couples in various stages of expressing their affection was the last thing he felt like encountering.

He was beginning to regret accepting Richard Palmer's invitation to go up to the shires for the hunting. He should have insisted that they go further away. Scotland perhaps. Or further. Somewhere that wasn't full of matchmaking mamas who had miraculously heard the news already.

"Wellington should employ a battalion of town tabbies to carry information for him," he informed the statue confidentially. "They could get a line on Boney's plans before he's even thought them."

It had only been two weeks since Muriel St. James had called off their engagement, but somehow everyone, even in this provincial backwater, seemed to know. The sly sympathy, the bawdy raillery—he didn't know which was worse. But of course either was preferable to the gaggle of beauties that had been paraded before him every afternoon and evening since he arrived. Apparently, any excuse would do for every woman in Lincolnshire to drag her unmarried daughters, trussed up in all their finery, to be entered into the grand Future Lady Iverley competition.

"No, my boy"—he patted the Cupid on the head— "I'm afraid you and I are now sworn enemies. Besides, I'm certain you have plenty to do, what with all that shrubbery."

"Who are you talking to?"

Iverley swung around. A female. Of course. And another pretty one. He wondered if her mama was lurking behind a tree nearby. He heaved a sigh of resignation. "I was talking to this statue of a fat, flying baby."

"Cupid."

"Yes. Cupid." Through the French doors he could see Richard and the rest of his friends making a move toward the card room. Cards would be a pleasant diversion. They would exempt him from dancing anyway. But the girl was standing on the steps, blocking his way.

"Lord Iverley," she said in a bright, nervous voice. And then, when he showed no signs of recognition: "We met two weeks ago. Well, actually, it was twelve days ago. If you count today." Her teeth flashed in a hesitant smile. "On Bond Street. I—I'm Richard Palmer's sister Georgiana." She gave a tittering laugh. "I daresay you don't remember me."

"Of course I do," he lied. "Richard Palmer's sister Georgiana." He did vaguely recall that Richard had a sister. This one might very well be her. She had the same dark hair and slight build as Richard did, anyway.

Her striking blue eyes were large in her face. It was a pretty enough face, small-featured and pointed, like a pixie. Yes, very pretty, actually. But he had no need for pretty.

"You were holding a black umbrella. Because it was raining." She twisted the fingers of her gloves and made a wry face. "That could describe any number of days. Or any number of people, I suppose. But it was raining, and you were trying to keep a package dry."

He remembered her now. He'd been on his way back from the tailor's when he'd run into Palmer and his sister. He hadn't realized then that he'd have no need for the wedding clothes he'd had fitted. He had a vague memory of a girl who had stared at him with a stunned, almost imbecilic expression in her wide, blue eyes. In all fairness, he hadn't remembered she'd been beautiful.

"How pleasant to see you again," he said, when she showed no signs of moving. He half expected a nearby hedgerow to extrude a sharp stick, prod the girl, and hiss some motherly advice.

"Yes!" she agreed with enthusiasm, violently wrenching the fingers of her gloves. "I hadn't expected to see you again so soon. How very lovely that you came here with Richard." She cleared her throat and again gave that high, nervous laugh. "He says that the hunting is very good here. My other brother William says so, too." She took the fan that dangled from a ribbon at her wrist and plied it with such vigor that her hair began to ruffle out of its pins. "Perhaps you know William?"

At his negative response, and the silence that followed, she looked daunted, then rallied and launched ahead. "No, I didn't expect you would. He doesn't much run with the sporting set. Though I believe you were at Oxford together. But he's three years older than you and Richard, and he's very serious. I daresay he spent most of his time there studying. Do you like poetry?"

"Poetry?" he repeated, blankly.

The flapping fan flew out of her hands and catapulted past his head. "Oh dear!" she exclaimed. "I'm so sorry. I don't know how I came to be so clumsy."

He leaned over and retrieved it. "Don't give it a thought." There was another strained silence, during which he wondered how he would medically aid her if she were to twist her fingers off entirely. "I'm afraid I have to go meet someone now," he said at last. He looked down to see that he still held her fan. On it was painted another representation of Cupid. Arch enemy.

"Here." He snapped the fan closed and handed it to her. It would be much better to repair to the card room, where the only hearts would be pips on the cards. As he passed her, he was vaguely aware that the scent she wore was appealing. Orange blossoms? It didn't matter. Merely another medium of female entrapment.

The tenacious creature followed him up the stairs. "I asked about poetry, because I am reading the most delightful book of verse by Cowper. I could loan it to you—"

He turned back to her. "My dear Miss Palmer, I'm afraid any attempt to introduce me to the finer, more civilized aspects of life will be lost on me. I intend to spend the rest of the autumn in mindless indolence. And unless you mean to spend your time hunting, driving, racing, shooting, and in general behaving like your brother Richard, I doubt very much that our paths will cross again." He attempted a smile but must not have succeeded, since Miss Palmer's face reflected sudden sympathy. "You will excuse me," he said stiffly.

He had a fleeting glimpse of her crestfallen expression before he beat a hasty retreat to the card room.

"Hullo, Iverley." Richard looked up from the table and grinned. "Where have you been?"

"In the garden. I met your sister," he added in a tight voice.

"Which sister, Georgiana or Emily?" His friend laughed at his bewildered expression. "Did she throw herself at your head?"

"Well, I—"

Richard fanned through his cards and discarded one. "Must have been Georgiana. Nice to know some chits still appreciate you, eh?" At Iverley's scowl he seemed to belatedly realize what he had said. "Oh well, dash it all. You know what I mean. Probably the best thing that could have happened, Miss St. James giving you the mitten like that. Brass tacks to Bond Street, she would have rung a peal over you for going hunting all autumn. She'd expect you to trundle up to see her family or some such rot."

"Most likely." Iverley slumped into a chair and pressed his fingers to his eyes.

"And she'd really have squeaked over us going to the fight next week. The ladies hate that sort of thing. Better off not to get buckled at all. A year from now, I'd wager you feel like sending her a letter of thanks for throwing you over. Stay unencumbered."

Iverley sank lower in his seat. "Unencumbered," he repeated like a vow.

Richard played a hand or two. "And mind my sister," he said with an offhanded gesture. "Georgiana's utterly bookish, and it's put all kinds of romantic notions in her head. She's good fun, and I'm dead fond of her, of course, but she's got her sights on you. Hasn't stopped nattering about you since she met you. Thinks you're perfect. A paragon of men." He rolled his eyes.

"She'll get over it."

"Unfortunately she's as stubborn as the devil himself," Palmer said with a laugh. "Quiet little thing. You wouldn't think she'd be the least bit of trouble at all, but once she gets an idea in her head, there's no calling her off it." He shook his head sadly. "She generally gets what she sets out to get, I'm afraid."

Iverley felt a tingle of alarm sweep through him. He had no intention of shackling himself to anyone, least of all some nervous creature with a tendency to throw things at him and spout on about poetry. "Tell her I'm not interested in the muslin company these days," he said. "In *any* of the muslin company."

"I have. Hasn't done a whit of good." He thought for a moment, his mind obviously more on the cards than his friend's predicament. "I likely shouldn't mention to her that Miss St. James jilted you." Palmer was oblivious of Iverley's wince. "She'd likely feel sorry for you. You know how chits who read novels like to think they can mend your broken heart. Perhaps I'll tell her you've already had your heart mended by someone else."

He didn't care what Richard told his sister. He just wanted to be rid of her. Rid of anyone who was going to look at him with that gut-wrenching look of admiration. He'd been duped once, and he wasn't likely to fall for female wiles again. Muriel had looked at him with a hungry expression, as though she could not bear to be without him. He realized now it was the same look she wore when she spied a fine Italian silk or a particularly fetching bonnet.

"Tell her anything," he said in a grim voice. "Tell her I hate novels. And poetry," he added with a faint, humorless smile. "Tell her we are ill-suited in every respect. I'm an inveterate sportsman who will likely care more for my cattle than for my wife."

Richard laughed his good-natured laugh. "I'll call her off if I can. I'm only her brother, so you know she won't listen to me." He looked up from his cards and sobered. "Honestly, Iverley, be kind to her. Not too kind, mind you. I've no desire to have you for a brother-in-law. But she's a good creature, and I'd rather you didn't break her heart."

Iverley stared into the fire and tried to wipe the image of her admiring expression from his mind. He hadn't done anything to deserve it, so it was obviously artificial. She was a better actress than most, but she was just the same in her motivation.

"I won't break her heart," he muttered to her brother. "I won't have anything to do with her."

Three

Georgiana pressed herself against a marble pillar in the entryway and wished she could become invisible. Couldn't the carriage be brought around more quickly? She wanted nothing more than to escape the scene of her humiliation.

What had she been thinking, babbling about poetry and black umbrellas? Iverley had looked at her as though she were a half-wit. She would never have the courage to face him again.

"Why the expression?" asked Richard, coming to her and putting her cloak over her shoulders.

"No reason. I'm merely tired. Are Mama and Emily ready to go?"

She'd gone about it all wrong. She'd raced out to find the man with no idea of what she would say. Somehow she'd had the ridiculous notion that she would have to do nothing more than present herself, and Iverley would look up with an expression of surprise and adoration, and take her into his arms.

"I won fifteen pounds at hazard," Richard volunteered, shaking out his own greatcoat. "Which is saying quite a lot, considering the chicken stakes we're made to play for at these assemblies." He rolled his eyes. "They're always such a dead bore. I shouldn't have told Iverley to come. Made me look like I hadn't a notion of how to entertain a fellow."

"I'm glad you brought him," she said quickly, then dropped her eyes to avoid her brother's speculative gaze. "That is, I know he's a particular friend of yours," she added.

Didn't Iverley know they were fated? How could he have looked at her with that expression in his eyes the first time he had met her, and not know? She couldn't be mistaken. Fate didn't play tricks on one like that. They were meant for each other. She couldn't just throw away her future after one slightly awkward encounter.

"Yes, I thought I would drag him out here for a bit of hunting this autumn," Richard said. "Wanted him to stay at Coningsby Hall with us, but he insisted on an inn." He flicked open the lid of his snuffbox, closed it, and then flicked it open again. "Does this look natural, Georgie? The catch is a bit stiff, and I feel like a fool struggling with it.

"Ah well," he said, returning to the subject of Iverley, "probably for the best he didn't stay at the house, or Mama would be boring him by wanting to show him her dashed bird drawings, and Emily would go on and on about her Season. And you"—he pointed an accusing finger in her face—"you would spend the whole time looking at him with that expression you're wearing right now."

"What expression?" She attempted to blank her face.

"The mooncalf one," he replied with a teasing pinch on her cheek.

She threw a glance toward the card room. So she'd looked like a mooncalf. She'd made a mull of it, but it was only because she'd gotten nervous. Perhaps Iverley had been nervous too. Or perhaps he was not ready to face what Fate had decided.

She had still felt it. Just like the first time they had met, she had felt the pull between them. When his eyes were upon her, she had felt like his whole attention was focused on her. It was as though he could see into her. The warm trembles she felt were more than attraction. Attraction was for those who knew nothing of each other. This was the fiery heat of Destiny.

"Listen, mooncalf, if it's Iverley you want, just forget it," Richard said in a confidential undertone. "He's a great gun, but he's just not for you."

She pretended to be absorbed in fastening her cloak. "Why do you say that?"

He nudged her arm. "Ah, now, don't take on. I don't mean you're not good enough for him. It's only that you're . . . you're too different. He needs a girl who likes hunting and driving and things like that. Not some vaporish miss who takes on if he wants to go shooting grouse instead of doing the pretty at some dull ball."

"I'm not vaporish," she said with some indignation.

Richard paused in putting on his own coat. "Didn't say you were. But really, Iverley doesn't care about books or music or all those things you like. You're chalk and cheese, the two of you. Let Iverley marry some bran-faced country girl who won't go all to pieces when he forgets her birthday. You go and marry someone more . . . more . . ." He searched for the word.

"More like Cousin Elliot?" she supplied dryly.

He appeared to consider her suggestion for a moment. "I suppose he'd do. A bit of a man-milliner if you ask me, but I suppose he wouldn't mind the poetry rot. Ah"——he looked up——"here's the carriage. Now where is Emily? Blast it if she isn't off eating all the ices or making an idiot of herself by asking men to dance. Don't know why Mama allowed her to come."

Georgiana moved toward the front door without really hearing him. Perhaps Richard had a point. Perhaps Iverley would prefer a woman who rode and drove and didn't give a rap for sentiment. Iverley had said very nearly the same thing himself: If she wanted to see anything of him, she'd have to act like Richard.

"William is coming down from London next week," her brother was continuing. "He's always good fun. So there will be plenty to think about besides some man you've nothing in common with."

"That will be lovely. We haven't seen him in months," she replied, somewhat absently. Their oldest brother was not the Corinthian that Richard aspired to be, but he enjoyed an autumn of hunting and shooting like most of the men in the county. With so many sportsmen around, Iverley could ride and hunt to his heart's content and would have no need to come to their modest country assemblies for company.

She felt a wave of frustration. Why hadn't she ever learned to hunt? She and Iverley could have spent the whole autumn together. He would have seen quite easily that Fate had meant for him to be with her. But now he'd spend all his time with the rest of the sportsmen, and he would never need to give her a second thought.

Her spinning thoughts lurched to a stop. And what was preventing her from taking up hunting now?

"Yes, Will's good fun," Richard agreed. "He and Iverley were at Oxford together, though they were a few years apart. Iverley's needle-sharp. Never got sent down like most of us. Not quite so longheaded as

Will," he said, pulling a face. "You and he got all the bookish tendencies."

"What kind of books does he like?" she asked, delighted to find this new facet to him. She had known it would work out.

"Will?" Richard looked confused.

"No, Iverley."

"Oh, I don't know! Books about sporting most likely." Her brother's eyes narrowed in a look of suspicion. "Iverley's here to get *away* from women. You likely haven't heard, but he was just thrown over by Miss Muriel St. James. You recall her; she drives a bang-up black gelding with the most magnificent gait. Iverley picked it out, of course. Grand animal. I'm sure he's kicking himself now for not keeping it for himself. He could have matched it with one of his own and had a spectacular pair. But of course Miss St. James can't drive a pair, and he can't very well ask for the animal back, now can he?"

Georgiana's skin went hot then cold. Iverley engaged to someone else? It seemed impossible. He couldn't have been; he was meant for her. Imagine if he'd married the wrong woman! She tried to calm her suddenly racing heart. But Fate hadn't let that happen. It was a sign, she knew it. She had one chance to have him, and she must take it.

Richard paused, looking as though he had suddenly recalled something. "However, I'm quite certain that any broken heart he *may* have suffered in the jilting is now quite mended."

She made a noise of assent and nodded vacantly. Her thoughts were running downhill, faster and faster, growing into an avalanche.

She could take up hunting. She could take up all things Corinthian. It would be the easiest thing in the world. She was perfectly capable of learning how to have interests in common with Iverley. Since they were fated to be together, she would likely find that they were fated to like the same things. It was only a slight inconvenience that she had never learned any skills befitting the wife of a noted sportsman.

She smiled, well pleased. It would require a little effort on her part, but it would all work out beautifully.

"What are you thinking, Georgie?" Richard said in a censorious voice. "Your chin is sticking out. And the only time you put your chin out is when you are determined to get your own way about something."

She smiled innocently, careful to ensure that her chin was back in line. "Don't be silly. I'm merely anxious to go home."

"Because I'm quite certain Iverley has no need of any female heart-mending nonsense. His engagement to Miss St. James was not what you would call a love match."

Of course it wasn't. She felt a momentary sense of gratitude that Miss St. James had had the foresight to see that her relationship with Lord Iverley was not meant to be. "Ah, here are Mama and Emily." She smiled, ignoring her brother's look of suspicion. "Shall we go?"

She stepped into the carriage feeling more cheerful than she had all evening. It was all settled. She would hunt this autumn. She would shoot; she would drive. She would learn to be everything Iverley wished for in a wife. If he only spent more time with her, he would realize that they were destined to be together.

And there was certainly no harm in trying to spend more time with him. It wouldn't be as though she were lying to him. She would only be helping Fate along.

Four

Georgiana came down the stairs, beating an energetic tattoo with her riding crop against the stiff skirts of her pale gray habit.

Richard paused in straightening his cravat in the hallway mirror. "Going riding?" he asked in some surprise.

She plucked the riding hat from his head and set it on her own. "I'm going hunting."

"Hunting?" he echoed. He peered under the brim of the hat, where it fell low over her eyes. "I didn't know you liked hunting."

"Well I like it now," she said. "And I'm going to ride out with you." She'd never actually been hunting, but goodness, how hard could it be? She was a fine rider, so what was the difference whether or not one rode in the direction of a small, woodland animal?

Richard seemed to consider her determined expression. "Very well. But don't come crying to me when you get thrown. Are you thinking to ride Woodsprite?"

"Of course."

Her brother reclaimed his hat and crammed it onto his own head. "Well don't. She's a fine saddle mare, but she's no hunter. Better take one of mine. Orion should suit you. Too small for me anyway." He looked her up and down and made a face of doubt. "Don't say I didn't warn you."

She took his arm and led him toward the stables. "Nonsense. It will be great fun."

Richard suddenly stopped in his tracks and narrowed his eyes. "You're not doing this just to play up to Iverley, are you?"

"Of course not," she replied, settling the wide cuffs of her gray riding gloves. "I merely thought that since I live in prime hunting country, I should learn to hunt."

He looked unconvinced. "Well I daresay that's for the best. Iverley's dead off females at the moment. And he's likely to think you're a complete ninny if you trail around after us complaining all day."

"I won't," she said with assurance. "I know just what I'm doing."

When they rode up to the group of sportsmen who had gathered on Lord Hennings's broad front lawn, she did not feel quite as confident. A half-dozen men were engrossed in a serious discussion of fox hunting strategy, while a few more limbered up their mounts by cantering them back and forth across the grass. A pack of hounds raced about underfoot in a frenzy of excitement.

Lord Iverley trotted over on his big black hunter. When he recognized Georgiana, his eyes widened in unmistakable surprise. "Miss Palmer, do you hunt with us today?"

"I—I thought I would try it." She heard her voice go high with nervousness, and resisted the urge to cringe. Why was it that every resolution she had to be cool and collected flew entirely out the window when he looked at her? Something in his penetrating expression put every rational thought out of her head.

"Georgie's game for anything," Richard put in generously.

Iverley's smile was strangely bland compared to the intensity of his gaze. "Well, I'm certain you'll enjoy it." He abruptly wheeled his horse around and rode off.

She tried not to feel disappointed, but reminded herself that the important thing today was to learn to like hunting. Everything else would fall into place. Fate would take care of it.

"Go easy and don't get underfoot," her brother continued his instructions. "The lads are likely to be cross if you muck things up by charging off when you don't know what you're doing." Richard's advice was cut short by the blast of a hunting horn. The drawers began beating the covert, and the riders followed. "Well, we're off. Remember"—he turned in his saddle to look at her—"no complaining."

They set off at an easy canter, following the pack of dogs that romped gleefully across the fields. For a long time the hounds seemed to be doing nothing but enjoying a good perusal of every stick and rock they came across, lolling and yipping in rough-and-tumble play.

Georgiana smiled up at the autumn sky and closed her eyes, enjoying the last warmth of the year. She had dreaded coming home at the end of the Season. She had thought at the time that it meant not seeing Iverley until next year. And even that hadn't been for certain, since Emily was to make her come-out in the spring. And even if Mama could afford to let her accompany Emily to London, Iverley might not be there, or he might be married already. The possible disasters were too numerous to mention.

She patted her horse's neck and picked up the pace

so that she wasn't lagging behind the pack. Now, everything was working out better than she had ever anticipated. Iverley would be here for the whole autumn. And if she took up hunting, which so far seemed simple, she could spend even more time in his company.

She was contemplating this pleasant prospect when one of the hounds set up a wild baying. It was soon taken up by his companions and in a moment every dog was streaking across the field, yodeling in triumph.

"Gone away!" Iverley exclaimed. And without a backward glance, he spurred his horse after them.

Georgiana followed, heeding Richard's advice to stay in the back and keep out from underfoot. True, she would like to impress Iverley, but it would hardly do to take a spill in front of him. She took the first two fences neatly, impressed with the ease with which Orion negotiated them. They went for what seemed like hours through fields and pastures, but the pack continued running at full cry. The riders began to stretch out behind them, the slower horses dragging behind as they followed the hounds up the steep hill toward a ridge of trees that marked the end of Hennings's land. Georgiana, dead last, clenched her teeth and pushed on in determination.

The fence at the edge of the wood was a heavy wooden affair, half fallen over and thick with thorns. Georgiana saw two men unseated as they attempted it. Lord Iverley's own animal balked and had to be taken at it again.

"It's easier down by the gate," he said shortly, indicating with a nod that she should take the fence there. His horse stopped short again, its nostrils flaring and its legs splayed.

Georgiana didn't give herself time to consider prudence. "Come on, my dear," she murmured to her mount. "Don't let me down in front of everyone." She patted Orion's neck and then spurred him toward the fence. He sailed over it with ease and continued following the whooping pack.

She was tempted to look back to see if Iverley had made it over the fence, but she was forced to concentrate on her riding. The hounds' cries had risen to a feverish pitch, and they seemed determined to lead the horses through every thicket of brush, icy stream, and pile of rocks they came across.

Orion came upon an embankment that had once been a fence, but was now a pile of rotted wood, thickly covered in ivy. The tendrils waved menacingly as they reached out toward the murky sunlight that filtered through the limbs overhead. Orion shied, then braced himself and took the fence.

Georgiana could hear the hunters getting further and further ahead. She ducked under a branch and then sat up, only to get slapped in the face by another. Her pretty gray hat with the curling red plume was dragged off her head. No complaining, she reminded herself, trying to determine which direction the hounds had taken.

The rise and fall of their howls were difficult to track. They seemed to come from everywhere in the dense woods and yet seemed to be continually getting further away. As she pushed onward, the branches grew lower and lower, blocking out most of the light. Orion slowed to a walk, picking his way through the brambles that thrived on the dark muddy floor of the forest.

"Why am I doing this?" she muttered. "To impress a man who doesn't even know I'm alive?"

She suppressed a shudder. The woods, when they entered it, had appeared to be a cool russet-colored glade. She had welcomed it, since it would mean the pack would be forced to slow. But now it seemed cold, almost menacing. She wondered if she would have to make an ignominious retreat back the way she had come. Or worse, face getting so lost that someone would have to be sent out to find her. The baying of the hounds continued to grow fainter and fainter. The stillness around her seemed to close in.

Then she heard a noise, a thrashing in the bushes, like a large animal coming toward her at a dead run. Orion threw up his head and pulled hard at the reins, but the creature in the woods kept pace with them, grunting with the effort as it plowed through the undergrowth. A boar? A stag? Whatever it was there was no getting out of its path.

All at once, the animal burst out the bushes, wild-eyed and snorting. It was a black horse. Orion shied out of the way before it slammed into them. The creature came to a stop, looking slightly bewildered, its empty stirrups dangling against its heaving sides.

Iverley's horse. But no Iverley.

"My lord?" she called out, tentatively. He must have fallen. Perhaps badly. She could see that his horse was limping slightly. "Lord Iverley?"

The faint hiss of the wind through the leaves sounded loud in the silence.

Georgiana pushed into the woods in the direction the horse came from. In the distance, she could hear the hounds wailing and the shouts of the huntsmen as they encouraged the dogs. "Iverley?" she called again. How would she get anyone's attention if he needed help? The pack must be half a mile away by now.

Perhaps he had been thrown somewhere else in the woods and the animal had wandered. She might never find him. The roar of blood in her ears made the sound of her voice seem small.

There was a bright splash of scarlet in the undergrowth. It must be Iverley's coat. She flung herself off her horse and waded through the brambles, which caught on her skirts and tried to hold her back. Good God, was he dead?

A wall, partly camouflaged by ferns and moss jutted up from a muddy trench. She could see the hoofprints where they'd slid in the stagnant water. "Iverley!" There was panic in her voice now.

She scrambled over the wall, fighting back the thorny whips of briars that grew up its flanks. Iverley still had not moved. Her heart was pounding in her temples as she slipped and struggled over the moss-slick stones.

He lay on his back, his pale face and red coat a startling contrast to the dark leaves. She threw herself onto her knees beside him. He didn't seem to be bleeding, but his eyes were closed, and he was motionless. Unconscious? Dead? No, that was impossible.

"Lord Iverley," she panted. "Can you hear me? Please say something."

Miraculously, his eyelids fluttered and his hazel eyes opened to look into hers. "Oh," he said in a flat voice. "It's you."

Five

Of all people to find him in this most humiliating situation, it had to be Miss Georgiana Palmer. He wondered if she'd start blushing and stammering and spouting on about poetry, when she should be doing something useful. Like pretending she hadn't happened upon him.

"Are you hurt?" she exclaimed, looking worriedly into his face.

Iverley wished she wouldn't lean so close. Pride aside, there seemed to be something sordid about lying on the ground with a beautiful young woman. Even if there was enough pain in his ankle to distract him from most licentious thoughts.

Most licentious thoughts. Miss Palmer looked nearly wanton with her hat gone, her hair pulled out of its pins and a smudge of dirt across her forehead. Instead of looking worse, the destruction of her prim chignon rather improved her. But still, she looked at him with an expression in her eyes that made something twist strangely inside of him. He closed his eyes to block out her face. "Oh no," he said cheerfully. "I just thought I'd have a bit of a lie-down."

"What happened?" she pressed.

"Gravity."

Her arched brows flattened into a look of faint irritation. "I'm only trying to help you. Shall I ride for the surgeon?"

He sighed and heaved himself onto his elbows. "No need for that. I'm only suffering the inevitable consequences of riding a new horse too hard and thinking myself invincible."

She offered her hand, and he took it, grudgingly glad of the help in rising. His ankle hurt like the devil, and he could feel the flesh beginning to press against the leather of his boot as it swelled. "I feel like a fool," he admitted, wondering why it irritated him that she was the one who'd found him. He should be glad to be reduced in her eyes. The last thing he needed was Palmer's slip of a sister trailing around after him. Her idol had been tumbled, most dramatically, and he should be relieved at the demotion.

She was brushing the leaves off his coat, scolding mildly. If Richard or one of the other men had found him, they would have laughed heartily, slapped him on the back, and taunted him for his folly in taking a green horse through such difficult terrain. He was rather more comfortable with that treatment than having a young lady stand entirely too close as she dabbed her handkerchief at the cut over his eye.

"Leave off," he growled, batting her hand away. "I can't stand being coddled. Just help me back on my horse, and we'll be off. It will take more than a tumble like that to kill me."

Miss Palmer stepped back and straightened her shoulders, a peculiar expression crossing her face. "I should hope so," she said with a faint smile. "You should have known that animal of yours would balk. There hasn't been a fence today he didn't object to."

There was something in her gruff tone that reminded him of her brother Richard.

To his surprise she put her handkerchief away, assessed him again with an eye that contained little sympathy, and turned away. He wished for a fleeting moment he'd allowed her to coddle him just a little more.

She started to climb back over the fence to where her horse was gingerly picking at weeds. He made to follow her, but nearly fell again when he put weight on his injured ankle. Miss Palmer looked back at the sound of his muttered curse.

"How did you manage to wrench your ankle? It seems much more likely that you would have gone headfirst." She returned to him and tucked herself under his arm. "If you're going to take a spill, you should at least make it a dramatic one. No one is going to feel the least bit sorry for you if you have nothing but a sprained ankle."

Without the least bit of maidenly fuss, she put her arm around him and supported him as he hobbled over to a low point in the wall. She helped him over it in the most businesslike way, without even the slightest hint of a nervous giggle.

"And any sympathy you gain for it will be eclipsed by the pity everyone will feel for you for having bought such a pathetic horse," she continued.

Did Richard have twin sisters? Who was this creature? She didn't seem in the least bit like the fluttery shy creature he had met last night. His friend had merely been bamming when he'd said his sister had a *tendre* for him. Richard's vulgar idea of a joke, most likely.

Miss Palmer continued her raillery, apparently oblivious to the fact that she was pressed against his side with her arm wrapped tightly around his waist. He should have shifted away from her, but he found that he could not walk without her support. He leaned on her, trying to ignore the tickle of her hair beneath his chin and the smooth roundness of her shoulder under the wool of her habit.

"Well, up you go. I daresay you'll be much happier riding than walking." She cocked her head and listened. "It sounds like they've called off the hounds. I wonder if that means they've got the fox."

He listened. "No, they've called them off because they lost the scent. A blank day. A fine end to your first go at hunting." There was something unsettling about being so close and trying to have a normal conversation. Even when waltzing, he'd never been so close to Muriel St. James. And here he was pressed hip to hip with Richard Palmer's sister.

She didn't seem to notice, but was considering his horse with her mouth pursed in thought. "Here. You'll have to mount from the wrong side. You won't be able to stand on your bad foot if you try to do it right way around. I'll give you a shove so you can get your leg over without too much weight on your bad ankle."

Her eyes were so incredibly blue, the blue of a tonic bottle. The blue of Tony Pawson's racing curricle. His eyes moved to her mouth, then he blinked and turned away. Better to think about Pawson's racing curricle.

She helped him hobble over to his horse and held the stirrup while he fitted his throbbing foot into it. There was no way he could lift himself into the saddle without putting weight on it. He drew a breath and prepared for the pain. Miss Palmer put one hand under his arm and the other under his thigh.

Surprise and desire clashed violently in his veins. "Miss Palmer, I believe I can—"

"Don't get missish on me," she snapped, giving him an upward shove that let him launch himself into the saddle.

He *was* getting missish, he mused, watching her calmly mount her own horse. Richard's joke in telling him that his sister had set her cap for him had made him vain. It was merely his puffed-up sense of self-consequence that had made him remember her as a blushing and stammering creature who stared at him with adoration in her eyes.

And it was merely the fall that had addled his own wits.

She rode out of the woods ahead of him, keeping up a stream of conversation about hunting and horses. His ankle throbbed painfully, but he focused on answering her questions as matter-of-factly as she asked them.

"Thank you," he said suddenly, interrupting her discourse on the virtues of the horse Richard had loaned her.

She turned to him in surprise. "For what?"

"For helping me." He felt like a bit of a fool and wished he hadn't broached the subject. If it had been one of his male friends who had aided him, he would not have felt the need to thank him. Since when had he become interested in drawing room manners?

She shrugged. "I would have helped you more by advising you not to ride that clumsy cart horse."

He'd been about to apologize for his rudeness last night in the garden, but he stopped himself in time. Whatever malady had possessed her then seemed to have passed, and her good sense seemed to have returned. In fact, now that she had stopped twittering he found he rather liked her.

"There they are," she said as they emerged from the

trees. The huntsmen were gathered in a grassy dell, where they knotted together talking, while the dogs chased each other around the horses' legs. No sign of the fox. It must have spirited itself away at the last moment.

"Did you want to make up a grand story of your mishap? Perhaps tell them you were wounded in rescuing me from a marauding woodcock? A savage hare?"

He laughed. "I shall tell them that you unhorsed me and then pummeled me until I admitted my folly in scorning women hunters."

"An excellent idea."

They rode toward the group, and Richard hailed them. "There you are at last. I was beginning to think I should have to call you out."

Iverley felt heat rise up his face, and he laughed far too heartily. "It is my horse who should be called out. The creature threw me. Your sister happened upon me in my time of crisis."

Richard shrugged. "Excellent excuse. I accept it unquestioningly and attribute the gratuitous mud stains on your coat to the fall. I would recommend, however, that your produce a rather spectacular injury to allay my suspicions."

"I rode my horse over him after our passionate tryst," Miss Palmer said blandly.

Iverley stared at her, half amused, half horrified. He didn't know many women. He'd always been more interested in sporting than the petticoat set. But he'd been under the impression that wit was not considered a womanly virtue.

Miss Palmer was certainly not the woman he had thought. And she was certainly nothing like the other females he had met during the Season. Even Miss St.

James, paragon of her sex, had always conducted herself as a circumspect, well-bred, unimaginative young lady should.

He slanted a glance at Richard's sister. She was interesting, there was no doubt of that. And she'd certainly shown no signs of setting her cap for him. Richard had obviously told him the bouncer for a joke. And since Miss Palmer quite clearly had no interest in making him a conquest, there could be no harm in getting to know her better.

"Wise decision, riding over him," her brother was saying. "Keeps him from becoming impertinent. In all seriousness, Iverley, are you hurt?"

"Wrenched ankle is all," he said, ignoring its howling. Perhaps Miss Palmer could recommend something to ease it. Someone so sensible would certainly know all kinds of remedies. He opened his mouth.

"Well make sure someone sees to it," she said brusquely. "I'm off to see how the hunt went."

And without a backward glance, she rode off.

Six

"You rode off?" Emily exclaimed. "How very unfeeling!"

Georgiana put down her book of poetry and began buttering a piece of toast. "Well, at first I was very concerned for him, but I was getting all-over fluttery, and I could tell he was getting irritated with me. So I decided I would act like Richard."

"Why?" her sister demanded, with a look of skepticism. "Richard is a jinglebrains."

"Oh, don't use that cant, Emily. It's dreadful." Mrs. Palmer swept into the breakfast room, tying on her bonnet. "I'm sure you picked it up from your brothers. I must speak to them about it. Are you certain you do not wish to accompany Emily and I, Georgiana? Mrs. Colbourne has a lovely new selection of muslin."

"He calls me a jinglebrains. I don't see why I can't call him one," Emily muttered.

Georgiana shook her head at her mother's invitation and went back to her book. Perhaps she'd overdone it. Or perhaps she hadn't been bold enough. It had been hard to tell if her plan was working. After all, one could hardly expect Iverley to fall into her arms after one encounter with the new Georgiana. But at least he had not looked at her with that expression of polite resignation. At least he had looked at her like he was really looking.

"Why in heaven's name did you decide to act like Richard?" Emily asked in a low voice as their mother went to collect her pelisse. "Our brother is hardly the model for womanly behavior. He's a . . . a . . ."

"Jinglebrains," Georgiana supplied. She closed the book with a pop. "Don't you see? Lord Iverley doesn't want a model of womanly behavior. He doesn't want a woman at all." It all made such perfect sense now. If she was everything he wanted, how could he resist her?

Emily's brows rose. "Really? I always thought he was quite—Well, really, Georgie, if he doesn't want a woman there isn't much point in chasing after him."

Georgiana collapsed back into her chair. "No, no, no. That isn't what I meant. I mean, after being jilted by Miss St. James, he is very wary of being in the company of ladies. What he wants is a friend, a crony. Someone he can go hunting with and talk about horse racing with. Someone who won't coddle him or flirt with him."

"So you are going to find out what he likes to do, and then become an expert in it," Emily said, suddenly enthusiastic. "I think it's a brilliant plan. And Richard can tell you everything about what he wishes for in a woman and then you can become it!" Then her face fell. "I don't think Mama would approve. She very much has her hopes pinned on Quigley. Being that he's a duke and all."

"Iverley is the man I was meant to marry," Georgiana said, suddenly fierce. "And if I have to go hunting every day, learn the names of all the racehorses and prize fighters in England, and pretend I don't care if he breaks every bone in his body, I will do it."

"I suppose," her sister granted. "But I don't know how you plan to keep it up. If you act like Richard, he'll start to think of you like he thinks of Richard, and then you will never wring a proposal out of him."

"Nonsense. He will come to see that I am the perfect match for him."

Emily gathered up her reticule. "I don't know, Georgiana. It sounds like a good deal of trouble to go to for a man."

"He isn't just any man," she said, almost to herself. "He's Lord Iverley."

Once her sister had left the room, Georgiana reluctantly put down her book of poetry and took up the sporting pages of the *Weekly Dispatch*. If she wanted to seriously make an effort to attach Iverley's interest, she would have to make a study of it.

The racing news she could understand well enough. Some of the owners and trainers were neighbors in Lincolnshire, so it was interesting to see their standing against the other contenders.

There was a long article on the art of pistol making, which was far too technical for her taste, but she plowed through it anyway. Feeling slightly foolish, she took out a pencil and began making notes in the margin. Very well, Iverley need never know how unnatural this was for her.

She read on. The news about the upcoming prizefight was next. It took her a few lines to realize that "the Fancy" was not a pugilist, but a term for the boxing world in general. The pages were graced with several drawings of the shirtless contestants wearing little else but ferocious scowls as they posed in various athletic attitudes. She felt vaguely as though she were attempting to read another language. The article was embellished with cant terms and expressions she could only guess at. She made a little dictionary along the top of the page, puzzling out the words' meanings from the context.

Richard entered the breakfast room and collapsed into a seat at the table. Georgiana looked up in surprise, and realized that several hours must have passed. Her tea was cold, and the sunlight that had originally lit a square on the wall now sliced across the table.

"Good God, Georgie, what have you been doing?" He looked at her with an expression of horror.

"Nothing. Just reading." She dropped the sporting pages into her lap and tried to look innocent. He would howl with laughter if he knew what she'd been up to.

He laughed anyway. "You look a fright. It looks like you've combed your hair with a hedgehog."

Georgiana realized she'd reverted to her old schoolroom habit of clutching a fistful of hair in her hand to help herself think. She made a futile attempt to repair the damage.

"Have you been cleaning the grate? Your fingers are all black and you've smudges on your forehead."

She examined her hands. "Newsprint. And pencil lead, I suppose. I was reading the paper."

He snatched the sporting pages from her lap. "Reading? It looks like you were trying to memorize the dashed thing." Comprehension dawned in his eyes. "You were—"

"Oh, don't say anything, Richard!" she pleaded. "You can be cross with me for ruining your newspaper, but don't say anything else."

He looked at her for a moment with an expression of perplexity. "Well, Will turned up late last night. He'll have brought another copy with him," he said mildly at last.

Her brother went over to the sideboard and examined the morning's offering. After loading his plate with buttered eggs and beefsteak, he balanced it carefully back to the table. For a while he seemed content to read the unmutilated portion of the paper and eat his way steadily through the plate of food.

"So, how did you enjoy the hunt yesterday?" he asked, just when she thought he'd drop the subject. "I saw that you caught your quarry, anyway." He raised his brows in a most insinuating manner.

Georgiana reluctantly pulled herself away from Cowper. "Oh don't be dreadful. It wasn't as though I engineered his fall. And I couldn't very well leave him, when I was the one who found him. I did what anyone would have done, so there's no need to look at me as though I plotted it." She poured her brother a cup of tea and refreshed her own cup. It hadn't been an entirely bad thing that Iverley had taken a fall. Perhaps now that he was convalescing she could visit him.

She indulged in the momentary vision of herself reading poetry to him while he lay on the sofa with his ankle wrapped in cotton wool. Surely once they spent more time together, he would realize how much they already had in common. There might be no call to air her recently acquired knowledge regarding the state of the pheasant population.

"I did enjoy hunting," she mused aloud. "It was much more difficult than I thought, though. And I was rather relieved that the fox escaped."

Her brother sorted through the mail, examining several invitations with distaste. "More interminable parties. I thought we'd be through with them now that the Season's over. I'm not going, anyway. It's outside of enough to be dragged to Almack's every spring. Wish I'd had more brothers instead of so many sisters. Thank heavens William's come up from London. He can do the pretty for a while, and I won't have to go."

Georgiana traced a finger around the rim of her tea-cup. "If you did have more brothers, what would you do with them? I mean, what is it that men like to do?"

Richard stopped in mid-chew and regarded her quizzically. "Damned bizarre question," he said through a mouthful of sausage. "Most of what men like to do can't be mentioned in front of ladies."

She frowned into the cup. "Yes, well, I was thinking more along the lines of things men wish women knew more about."

He laughed. "Most of that can't be mentioned either." He went back to eating and perusing the mail. "Sports," he said after a long pause. "Horseracing, boxing, anything you can bet on. It would be nice to have a rational conversation with a chit about that. Anything other than how fine or not fine the weather is, or how lovely the party is, or how-do-you-like-Lon-don-Mr. Palmer."

"Oh. And poetry? Books?"

He thought for a moment. "No. Can't say that I ever want to have a conversation with anyone about that, girl or not. It might be interesting"—he looked thoughtfully up at the ceiling—"to be able to talk about plays, as long as it's only the farces and certainly not about opera, unless you're making fun of the sing-ers." He went back to buttering toast and reading a letter propped up on his teacup. "And it would be pleasant to meet a chit who one could tell a joke to without her getting all over horrified. For instance, I heard one about a girl named Peg—Oh!" He nodded at the letter. "Iverley is asking after you."

A prickle danced over her skin. "Is he?" She cleared

her throat and tried to appear very absorbed in shaking the crumbs from her napkin.

"Said you were a great gun. Said we should go see him since he's laid up with his ankle."

A great gun? What was a great gun? She longed to snatch the sheet out of Richard's hand and look the words over herself. How exactly had he written them?

Richard was watching her with a peculiar expression on his face. "Well aren't you panting to go? I thought you were keen on him."

No, it was best not to reveal her plan. She had the faintly disturbing feeling that her brother would disapprove of her methods. "Oh dear me, no," she said with an airy wave of her hand. "I'm certain he's everything amiable, but I'm certainly not over the windmill for him. He's far too dashing for the likes of me."

Richard finished off his tea and pushed back from the table. "Discovered he wasn't perfect after all, did you? Well, it's likely for the best, and you won't waste your time ruining the newspaper with your scribbling. I told you, he's not the least bit interested in getting buckled after what happened in Town."

He made to leave the room, but turned back at the doorway. "Well, I think I'll head over to his lodging house. Cheer him up a bit." He thought for a moment. "Coming?"

Georgiana felt a cold wash of panic. She was still savoring her triumph of yesterday. How would she ever manage to keep up her façade of careless camaraderie day after day? She hadn't anticipated how tiring it would be to act the part of the dashing, neck-or-nothing sportswoman.

"Georgie?" her brother prodded.

"Yes, yes, I'll go. Just let me change my gown."

He sighed dramatically. "Well don't be forever

about it. This isn't like a morning call or any such thing. No sense in fancying up."

It took her far longer to pick what to wear so that she shouldn't appear to have taken much trouble over her dress than if she had tried to look her best. At last she descended the stairs wearing a plain wool gown with long, pointed sleeves from last Season. It wasn't anything remarkable, but it was a blue that matched her eyes and darkened her hair to nearly black.

Richard scolded her for her tardiness most of the way to Iverley's lodgings at the Crossgrave Arms, until she managed to distract him by asking to drive his team. He then blithely spent the rest of the journey instructing her how to handle his high-blooded pair. She pulled up in front of the inn well pleased with her efforts. Even her brother begrudgingly allowed that she had fine hands.

When they entered his room, they found Iverley reclining on a settee, his bandaged leg propped up on its arm. His coat was discarded in a heap on the chair. Georgiana's vision of him, tame, letting her read to him while he convalesced, flew out the window at the sight of his broad chest. She dropped her eyes and tried to swallow.

"Behold the wounded soldier!" Richard announced, tramping over to clap him on the back. "Mrs. Evans has been coddling you, I see." He nodded in derision at the bowl of gruel and glass of weak wine.

"Terribly," Iverley agreed. "I'm well nigh going mad cooped up in here. But until I can get my boots on, I'm not likely to make my escape."

"At least it will keep you from being expected to turn up at any of the dashed balls everyone keeps throwing. My mother must have gotten a half-dozen invitations today."

"We brought you the sporting paper," Georgiana blurted out without preamble. "Thought it might while away the time." She checked to be certain she'd brought William's clean copy of the paper and not the one she'd made notes on, then shoved it toward him.

His brows rose in a slightly bewildered expression. "Thank you, Miss Palmer. I don't get the paper here."

"Wouldn't have thought to bring it myself," Richard admitted.

"I had hobbled to the window when you arrived," Iverley said, looking slightly sheepish. "Quite anxious for company, I suppose. And I saw that you were driving, Miss Palmer."

She felt a flush of pride. Her plan was paying off even more quickly than she'd expected. "Richard is teaching me," she said, infusing her voice with nonchalance. "I drove a bit in London, but never a pair."

"She's a natural," her brother said with pride. "Excellent hands. I'd buy her a pair of her own, if I had the blunt. Which I won't until next quarter."

"By which time you will have forgotten." Georgiana smiled and turned back to Iverley. The autumn light from the window lit the auburn highlights in his hair. He looked like a statue of a reclining Roman god. He was still, but there was a look of acute assessment in his eyes. To her surprise, he turned his gaze on her. Then, before she could even get flustered, the expression was gone, and he had turned back to Richard.

"I plan on being up and about by the Sleaford race meet," Iverley said with a rueful smile. "Damned inconvenient being laid up on the first hunt of the Season. Begging your pardon, Miss Palmer," he added, realizing what he'd said.

"Don't mind her," Richard assured him. "She isn't a Bath miss about language."

She wished her brother was, perhaps, not quite so dismissive, but it was what she wanted, wasn't it? To be one of the lads?

"Whom do you favor?" she asked, trying desperately to remember the horses that were racing.

Iverley's brows jerked inward in an expression of perplexity that was quickly gone. "Well, Pig-in-Trousers is by far the favorite. But I know Jim Wells, and he's been training him too hard. Always does. His horses run well enough in the spring, but by these fall meets, they're all blown out."

"And Fatal Fancy?"

Again that expression. He looked at her for longer this time before answering. "A good goer. Depends on the turf. If it's dry, I'd say he has a good enough chance." He shifted to a sitting position. "I didn't know you followed horse racing, Miss Palmer."

"I . . . I don't," she admitted, feeling the wretched blush coming on. "I only listen to Richard when he's going on about it."

"You're the only one who listens," Iverley said, throwing her brother a look of pretend derision. "Sporting-mad he is. Not another thought in his mind."

"Say, Iverley?" Richard asked from the window. "Who owns that bay the groom is leading out in the yard just now? Fine shoulders. I daresay if you offered enough you could buy him. Give him that stumblekins of yours in the bargain, and you'd be a good deal better off next time you're out with the hounds."

She and Iverley exchanged a glance of suppressed humor. His boyish grin disappeared quickly, but it left behind a warmth like July. He had a ready wit, and if he could mock Richard's zeal, then perhaps there was more to him than the typical sportsman. Perhaps he could learn to like the finer things in life. Perhaps, someday, once they were married, she could admit that she loved books and plays and music, and he could learn to love them, too.

"And yourself?" she said. "Are you such the Corinthian that you think of nothing but sporting?"

He leaned back again in an attitude of despondency. "What a poor fellow you must think me, Miss Palmer. Lumping me in the same category as your brother. My interests are many and varied."

Hope flickered through her. Even if he didn't care for the things she liked, perhaps she could glean what she should be studying up on. "Oh certainly," she said with a daring attempt at archness. "If one includes pugilism, hunting, fishing, shooting, and driving, the list becomes enormously varied."

He looked out from under the hand he had thrown over his eyes. "Nonsense. Just because I do not care for poetry . . ." She saw a gleam of hazel eyes as he flashed her a teasing look. "It does not mean I am completely unappreciative of the finer accomplishments of man."

She was triumphant. Of course he would learn to love the things she loved. They were meant to be together. "You've still neglected to name them," she reminded him, dragging her eyes away from his face to watch Richard as he meandered about the room, examining the bowl of gruel and the vials of tisanes the landlady had provided.

Iverley rubbed his chin and affected an expression of intense thought. "I enjoy reading," he said after a moment. "Particularly history. I have been known to take pleasure in patching the roof of a house or mending a fence, if you can credit it." Though his negligent pose had not changed, his voice had grown more earnest. "I have an interest in seeing that my tenants' land is well farmed and that my heirs shall never have cause to complain that I spent all my time in idleness."

There was more to him than even she had credited him with. Of course he was handsome, and she had always known him to be everything gracious and charming, but there was a serious side to Vaughn Iverley she hadn't really expected. Her heart gave a strange, heavy beat within her.

"You're too perfect to be true." She realized with a painful blush of horror that she had said the words aloud. How could she have made such a stupid mistake? After all her carefully planned nonchalance he would brush her off as just another woman pursuing him.

"Well," he said in a different tone, after a pause, "now that I have assured you that I am indeed a person of more dimension than your brother here, I may go back to talking about hunting and coursing with impunity."

"Ah yes," she raced to cover her slip. "I would love to learn more about hunting. And coursing. And . . . and boxing," she added for good measure, ignoring Richard's expression of patent disbelief.

"Really?" said Iverley. "Palmer, I had no idea your sister was so sporting mad."

"I hardly knew myself," her brother said darkly.

"And you drive as well," he mused. "Really you must forgive me, but I thought at first that you were one of those young misses who minces about quoting poetry and getting sentimental about dewy flowers and things like that."

"I'm not!" Certainly she had no strong predilection for dew. "I don't give a rap about gossip or fashion or—or society nonsense."

Iverley propped himself up on his elbow. "You can't know how relieved I am to hear it."

"Oh yes," said Georgiana, warming to the topic, "I'm mad for sports and gaming. And, of course, Richard is teaching me to drive. Hopefully he'll teach me to shoot next."

"Oh certainly," her brother said with sarcasm. He pointed his finger down at Iverley's head from his position behind the sofa. "Thought you were off him," he mouthed silently.

"He is the *best* of brothers," she assured Iverley in a loud voice. Perhaps she was rather overstating her enthusiasm for hobbies she knew Iverley favored, but really, it wasn't a complete untruth. She didn't mind the idea of shooting or driving, anyway. She hoped Iverley didn't take up cockfighting or something else dreadful.

He smiled. "I came down here to get away from society, but I must admit that I wouldn't half mind it if there were more women who could be sensible like you."

She saw it. Just for a moment. It was that look she had seen when they had first met. It was gone in a moment, but she felt flushed, triumphant. It has been there.

Richard gave a snort, which she was obliged to cover by rattling the teapot as she poured out more tea. "Well," she said as she handed Iverley a steaming cup, "it is remarkable that we share so much in common."

Seven

Iverley watched his sister put the last touches on her elaborate headdress. She'd come down instantly upon hearing he'd been injured, despite the fact that he had insisted there was absolutely no need. But Caro had always loved to play the older sister, so he willingly indulged her coddling.

"I know what you're thinking," she said when she caught him watching her reflection in the mirror. "You think I'm a dreadful busybody to have come down here and spoil all your fun." She shot her brother a teasing look. "You're thinking I came down here merely because I was bored all by myself in the dreadful pit of a house Markham left me, and I'll want to be squired about to all the parties and gatherings, while what you really want to do is drink too much, eat too little, gamble away your money, and go to sporting events."

"Yes." He hid his smile. "That's a fairly accurate assessment."

She turned around and straightened his cravat for him. "When are you going to give up your bachelor ways and let someone else take care of you?"

He turned away from her, covering the rush of bitterness with a laugh. "Why should I ever do so when I have you to take care of me?" he said with forced lightness. He gave his neck cloth one last twitch, pretending not to see her look of sympathy. "Besides, your marriage was hardly an inspiration to me."

Caro smiled and rolled her eyes. "I make a very bad widow, I'm afraid. I can never remember to look devastated when people mention Markham. And really, it would be quite hypocritical of me to pretend to be truly upset that he's gone. After all, he was nearly twenty-seven years my senior, and we were only married for a year and a half."

"But at least you attained that holy grail of womanhood: marriage," he said, limping over to the mirror, where his valet was holding out his topcoat and walking stick.

Caroline scowled at him as she threw her evening wrap over her shoulders. "You have become a cold, cynical man since Miss St. James broke off your engagement."

He laughed, but it sounded false, even to his own ears. "Well at least she left me with something." His ankle was hurting him, and he didn't want to go to this silly ball. Why did Caro think he needed to be taken care of? It was good of her, but he wanted nothing more than to spend a pleasant autumn doing nothing but what pleased him, and instead he was plagued by well-meaning females who seemed to think he needed company.

Except for perhaps Miss Palmer. She alone seemed to understand that he'd rather talk about anything other than his wretched ankle, and that he didn't want someone asking him every other minute if there wasn't something she could do for him.

He reluctantly took his sister's arm and let her aid him down the stairs to the waiting carriage. Something in her eye suggested she was still thinking about his current unsatisfactory state of bachelorhood. "A very nice evening for a ball, I suppose," he said, though he didn't really know the kind of weather a ball required.

His attempt to divert her attention from the course down which it had wandered was futile. "Haven't you met any nice young ladies?" she prodded.

"Many."

"Any who are interesting?"

"No."

Caro's chin jutted out in an expression of annoyance. "Really, Vaughn, if you tell me that you are heartbroken over Miss St. James, I shall laugh in your face. A more conniving, social-climbing little cat I never saw."

He laughed and settled back against the squabs. "I'm not the least bit heartbroken," he agreed. "I'm also not the least bit interested in becoming entangled again. You look very well tonight. Are you looking forward to dancing now that you're out of mourning?"

"If I were to choose a woman for you," Caro continued, unswerving as a charging bull, "I would choose someone close to your age."

"I believe your own unhappy marriage quite vividly demonstrated the wisdom of that course," he said dryly. For some reason, he found himself calculating the age difference between himself and Miss Palmer. She couldn't be more than three or four years his junior.

How ludicrous that she should pop into his head. Miss Palmer was a tomboy, a neck-or-nothing female with no more interest in getting caught in the parson's mousetrap than he.

Caro tapped her chin with her fan, entirely oblivious of his presence. "She would be someone kind, not sophisticated and calculating like Miss St. James. I know you thought she was dashing, but someone less con-

cerned with society would be ever so much better."
Caroline smiled placidly at the roof of the coach. "And
someone with a sense of humor. You know Miss St.
James had none. Obviously someone of good family,
but not too high in the instep."

"A paragon."

"Someone clever," his sister continued, obviously
fully enraptured by the mental picture of his future
bride. "Someone who loves you for what you are."

Muriel had not given a rap for who he really was.
She cared far more about who *Debrett's* said he was.
His mind took him back to the afternoon in London
when he'd first met Miss Palmer. She'd not even
known his name, and she'd looked at him as though
he'd invented sunlight. That memory made his neck-
cloth feel tight and itchy. He liked Miss Palmer better
when she was acting like she had some sense.

"So far my mare Pepita fits the bill best," he said
with a glib shrug. "Except for the difference in our
ages, which I'm afraid is rather shocking."

His sister shot him a look of annoyance, as though
she'd only just noticed he was present. "I only want
to see you happy."

"And you don't mind if you make me miserable
doing it," he finished for her. "Leave off, Caro. I'm
off the muslin company for a while. When I'm good
and ready, rest assured that you will be the first person
I shall come to when I want advice on finding a wife."

The house at the end of the drive was a constellation
of lights. Carriage after carriage pulled up at the broad
white steps. Lord Oldstone must have invited all of
Lincolnshire. As they made their way up the steps,
Iverley could feel the rich, warm air full of smells and
music wafting out of the house into the night. He sud-

denly felt rather more charitable toward Caroline for forcing him to go.

They were received by their host and hostess and then made a slow circuit of the ballroom, greeting their friends and acquaintances. Iverley was looking forward to sitting down and playing cards for the duration of the evening. With his ankle just mending, he mercifully wouldn't be expected to dance.

He wondered if Georgiana Palmer liked to dance.

She and Richard had been over to see him nearly every day for the last week, and she seemed to have entirely gotten over her tendency to spout nonsense about poetry and stare at him with a strange expression on her face. She talked about horses, driving, and hunting like a sensible person. In fact, they shared an amazing number of interests. He didn't think he would mind dancing with her in the least.

His sister was looking longingly at the dance floor herself, so he looked around to find her a partner. Most of the men he knew here in Lincolnshire didn't know one country dance from the next and would doubtless fall into a panic were he to ask them to take his sister to the floor.

Across the room he saw Miss Palmer's brother, William. He recalled the man vaguely from his Oxford days. Will Palmer was always far more interested in study than in doing the pretty. Nonetheless, when William saw them, he detached himself from a group of scholarly looking men and came over to them.

"Forgive me for imposing, I—I don't know if you remember me," he stammered. The nervous expression on his face forcibly reminded Iverley of the time he had met Palmer's sister in the garden.

"Of course I recall you," he said, shaking William's

hand. "Richard speaks of you often, though I'm afraid we don't see you in London above much."

"No, I'm afraid not. I mostly travel the country looking for specimens. I'm writing a book on weeds."

"Weeds?" echoed his sister. "Not flowers or other plants?"

William laughed a little sheepishly. "No, my specialty is weeds. Very important to learn about. They have an enormous impact on all our crops, you know."

"Mr. Palmer, this is my sister, Mrs. Markham. Widowed," he remembered to add, just in case William cared one way or the other. "She's come to take care of me in my infirmity."

"A book," said Caro, her smile becoming admiring. "That must take an enormous amount of work."

"Richard is obviously the rattle of the family," Iverley put in with a laugh.

"Actually," said William, warming up a little, "it is interesting. Richard and Emily are very alike, outgoing and charming, very like my mother, while Georgiana and I tend to be reserved to the point of shyness." He blushed at the length and boldness of this speech.

Miss Palmer? Shy? He wondered if William had inadvertently mixed up his sisters' names. And where was she anyway?

"Do you dance tonight, Mrs. Markham?" William said, speaking to the floor.

Iverley made a mental note to thank him later for the favor. Once the assembly saw that Caro meant to dance tonight, she would not lack for partners. And perhaps Palmer could introduce her to a few of his learned friends. She would like that much more than spending the evening with his sporting cronies.

Caroline sensed his impatience and gave him a slap on the arm with her fan. "Go, you terrible creature," she said teasingly as she took William's elbow. "I know you wish to be off. I plan on behaving most shockingly now that I'm out of mourning, so I shall be glad to be rid of your company."

Iverley grinned at her and then limped slowly toward the card room. He saw several young ladies looking with regret at the walking stick he held and was again glad he wasn't expected to dance. He was in no mood for socializing and wanted nothing more than to take himself off to the card room, where his ill temper would be attributed merely to his losses at the table.

If William Palmer was here, his sister must be here as well. He wished momentarily he'd thought to ask William, but then realized it would have made him look overly anxious.

A mocking voice in his head noted that while he counted himself great friends with Miss Palmer's brother Richard, he never put himself to the trouble of walking around a party looking for him. But he continued to scan the room for Georgiana anyway.

The card room was crowded and stiflingly hot. From the back came the sound of raucous laughter. A waiter squeezed through the crowd with a tray of drinks, and Iverley relieved him of a glass.

A friend of Richard's hailed him and pointed to an empty chair at his table, but Iverley waved him off. For some reason he didn't feel inclined to play. He blamed it on his ankle, but the pleasant tingle of anticipation he had felt in coming up the drive had now sputtered down to a flat sense of boredom.

"Hazard, Iverley?" Lord Quigley suggested. "We're about to start a new round."

"No, thank you," he replied with a slight bow. "I think I'll take a turn around the room to see who's here first." It was far too hot. And the table in the back was exceedingly noisy. He considered for a moment going back into the ballroom. Perhaps Miss Palmer had been in the dining room or in the ladies' withdrawing room when he had arrived.

The realization that he was still looking for her irritated him still further.

Then he saw her, surrounded by people at the table at the back of the room. Hickham hung over her shoulder, leaning close to give advice. Both Sir Randolf and Lord Pawson were glowering at Hickham and trying to attract her attention on her left. The rest of the table was roaring with laughter over something she had said.

He limped closer and heard her laughing. "Yes, well I daresay Richard will be a good deal less smug about that jack he played when he learns I had bet his best hound on it," she said.

"Did you?" Richard roared, halfway between amusement and annoyance. "I know you only did it because you're cross I lost your earrings."

"What's all this?" Iverley asked. He meant to sound disinterested but failed.

"Grand game," Hickham replied, shuffling the cards with a dexterous flick of this thumbnail. "We've decided that the stakes will be each other's belongings. See, we each start out owning the property of the person on our right. Then we bet it based on what we think it's worth. Causes loads of rows, of course. And gets dashed confusing because, if you win, you have to remember all the things that were bet, because now they're yours. Hilarious fun. Much better than real money. Miss Palmer invented it."

"I see," said Iverley. "And how does one settle up in the end?"

"Don't quite know yet," he admitted. "But I expect I've lost my watch and my favorite waistcoat forever."

"Shall we deal you in?" Richard asked.

Iverley flicked a glance at Miss Palmer, but she had turned to talk to Mrs. Jonesborough. "Certainly," he said, settling himself carefully into a chair beside Pawson. "Though I can't say I particularly want all your possessions. I'm likely to be remarkably careless with them."

He wished, for a moment, that he were at the right hand of Miss Palmer. But that was ridiculous. A week ago he'd been wishing she'd leave off giving him that silly misty look. He must be more vain than he knew.

"Very well." Miss Palmer turned around briskly. "Ah, you have joined us, Lord Iverley." She smiled. "Tony, you must be very careful in your play now that Iverley owns everything. He has shown himself to have shockingly bad judgment." A dimple that he had never noticed before appeared next to her mouth. "Particularly of horseflesh."

"If you lose Flier, I shall have your hide," Pawson informed him.

Since when had Miss Palmer been on first-name terms with Pawson? "I shall be prudence itself," he said dryly.

"Since you have just joined us, my lord," Miss Palmer continued, "the rules are that you must only bet your neighbor's possessions that are smaller than a horse."

"Inclusive," added Richard.

"And less valuable. So I'm afraid there is no betting Tony's country seat, town house, sisters, or even his lovely blue curricle."

"Thank God," Pawson muttered.

"I understand entirely," Iverley assured her. While Sir Randolf dealt the cards, he looked around. The whole room seemed fascinated with the game, and as play started, the arguments and bantering that went around the table induced roars of laughter in the crowd gathered around. It was definitely a more amusing way to spend an evening than dancing attendance on the usual parade of simpering misses.

He watched Miss Palmer as she dealt the cards. Her arms were long and slim. They rose and fell, graceful, as though she were always dancing when she moved. It was mesmerizing.

Since when did he become poetic?

He forced his mind to examine her analytically. She played well enough, but seemed to derive much more amusement from wagering the most bizarre and comical items from her neighbor's belongings. Her memory for the imaginary items she had collected was prodigious, but he could see that she had no real passion for card playing.

Mrs. Jonesborough, who at present had custody of his own belongings, was instead an avid card player. She bet only his most obvious and valuable assets and kept a meticulous list at hand where she tallied the items she had won. A spirited argument arose over the legality of this memory aid, but her utter refusal to play if she was not allowed it settled the question.

"Lord Iverley?" Miss Palmer's voice drew him back from the amusing consideration of whether Miss St. James would have ever contemplated playing, much less inventing, such a peculiar game. "Mrs. Jonesborough has just bet your collection of Chinese snuffboxes, and you fail to look properly alarmed. Are we right to assume that they are either unimportant to you or utterly worthless?"

"My snuffboxes?" He recalled himself with difficulty. "Mrs. Jonesborough, you are vicious. It has taken me years to amass them." He examined his cards with an exaggerated expression of concentration. "Remind me what is at stake on the table?"

"Mr. Hickham has bet Sir Randolf's cherrywood escritoire," Miss Palmer said. "Lord Exeter has put in Hickham's subscription to the opera; Mr. Pawson bet the services of Exeter's valet; Richard, being singularly uncreative, put in Pawson's valet; Sir Randolf put in my entire collection of poetry, the wretch, which he won last round; I put in Mrs. Jonesborough's court dress, which the King himself particularly noticed the embroidery work on, and now it comes to you."

He hadn't been paying very much attention to the game. One of the advantages of betting other people's belongings was that it gave one plenty of time to think about other things and watch the players. Hickham, despite the fact that he was playing Sir Randolf's possessions, played gingerly and cautiously. Richard was sloppy as usual, and Pawson far more profligate than he ever would have been with his own money. And Miss Palmer was the center of all the merriment. Her raillery was not flirtatious; she didn't simper or talk nonsense. She played well, and she made certain that everyone was amused.

"Isn't she amazing?" Tony Pawson murmured as she listed off once again what everyone had bet this round.

Iverley scowled and wished that everyone at the table hadn't noticed that, indeed, she was. He looked at his hand once more. "I believe I own Richard's roan hack," he said at last. "I'll put that in."

"You are confident," she said with a smile. He found himself suddenly wishing that he would win her collection of poetry. Of course he would give it back to her, but it would be amusing to quiz her over its value.

They played a round, as in speculation. Miss Palmer turned up the ten of hearts and he, after heated dickering over the price, bought it.

"Oh, you rogue!" she cried, as he lay down his winning hand. "I should have known you had them all!"

"I do hope my valet isn't annoyed that I now have no less than two new, spare valets. I shall be changing clothes every hour just to keep them all occupied," he said mildly.

There was a disturbance in the crowd, and Lady Oldstone pushed her way to the table. "What are you doing?" she demanded, putting her finger in his face. "You're ruining my ball!" She was teasing, but there was a look of irritation behind the smile. "There is almost no one dancing, and if you knew the expense I went to to hire those musicians all the way from Lincoln, you would fair faint. Everyone is in here watching you play cards. I won't tolerate high stakes here, you know. This is no gaming hell."

"Ah, madam, I must beg your pardon. We have indeed been remiss," Iverley said.

"It is my fault," Miss Palmer spoke up. "I've allowed the game to go too far. Indeed, it is time we stopped. We should enjoy more of the marvelous entertainments you've arranged, Lady Oldstone."

"And I will lead the charge," he said, rising to his feet. "Miss Palmer, will you do me the honor of dancing?" He quelled the alarms ringing in his head by insisting to himself that he was merely being polite.

She was looking at him with a quizzical expression. "And carry you as you limp across the floor?"

He'd forgotten about his ankle. A flush rose up his neck. "Perhaps then you'll condescend to support me to the dining room for sustenance."

She looked at him with an inscrutable expression

that made him think for a rather humiliating moment that she was going to refuse him in front of everyone. Then her face relaxed. "I'd be delighted," she said calmly. Though he noticed that her dimple did not show when she smiled. There was a strange, almost worried expression in her eyes, almost as though there were alarm bells going off in her own head as well.

Eight

They made their way slowly to the dining room, their progress impeded by Iverley's limping gait and the number of people who now emerged from the card room and began filling the salons and corridors of the great house.

Georgiana said nothing. She couldn't remember the plans she had formulated. Something to do with being calm and detached. But as usual every time she was with Iverley, she felt the urge to throw herself into his arms and start babbling nonsense. She'd gotten better at hiding it these days, but her heart still went gallumphing about her body when he was near her.

"I admit, you have intrigued me, Miss Palmer," he said, as they made their way through the crowd on the stairs.

Walking closely by his side, she was reminded of the day he had been thrown from his horse. When she had been pressed tightly against him as she helped him to walk, she could almost feel what it was like to be embraced by him. She had had the strangest fancy that she could feel the warmth of his body and the beat of his heart under his coat.

Now again they were shoulder to shoulder. This time not so close, but the mass of the crowd seemed, paradoxically, to afford them an intimacy even greater than that day in the woods.

"Intrigued you? Why is that?"

"You play cards well, and certainly have a flair for innovation. I don't remember the last time I have enjoyed playing more. But I don't believe you enjoy it."

She looked at him in alarm and saw that his hazel eyes were assessing her. Did he know that she had only been playing because she knew he enjoyed it? "Of course I like cards," she said with a lift of her shoulders. "I admit though that I am not fond of losing, which I inevitably do. That was how I hit on the idea of playing with someone else's possessions. I thought that if someone else were betting for me, perhaps I should come out the winner."

His limp brought his shoulder in contact with hers every time he took a step. She should move away from him, but instead pretended she did not notice it.

The supper room was empty. Most people had already eaten and had gone back to the ballroom. Two elderly gentlemen sat snoring over their port and a boisterous set of young people she didn't know were laughing and chattering in another corner. The muffled sound of the music and conversation from the ballroom made the room seem strangely isolated.

She cast about in her mind for a subject he would find interesting. "Richard and William are off to the mill tomorrow. It's the talk of the town. Will your leg keep you from it?"

"Not in the least," he said, examining the feast laid out for them. "Will you go?"

He sounded almost eager. Joy sang through her like a harp string.

"Oh, I wish I could. Richard and Will won't have it though. I know it isn't the place for ladies, but I would so like to see Cribb in action." Not *precisely* true, but she did wish Iverley and her brothers weren't going off and leaving her behind. Besides, after all her research she wanted to see what all the fuss was about.

Iverley's brows rose slightly higher on his forehead at her reply, and she felt a momentary sense of panic. Perhaps Cribb, the only boxer's name she knew, wasn't fighting in tomorrow's mill.

But Iverley had already launched himself enthusiastically into the discussion. "He's an amazingly graceful man. And of course has about the best left hook this country's ever seen."

He went on for quite a while in this vein, and she nodded attentively, remembering not to let her gaze wander. Did he always smell this nice? She resisted the urge to reach out and touch the short, reddish brown curls at the nape of his neck.

"Richard says that it will be deadly dull, since Cribb's certain to take John Hill in the first few rounds," she put in. "But I'm not so certain. Hill has stamina that can wear Cribb down." She riffled urgently through her mental notes. "Do you remember how he went thirteen rounds with the Molyneaux last May? If he can only manage to keep out of Cribb's way, Cribb will beat himself." She nodded sagely and helped herself to a tissue-thin slice of ham. "Oh, don't bother filling a plate for me. You're wounded and of course I'm capable of doing it myself. It's only me, you know, not some London lady."

"I can still be polite to you," he objected, trying to take her plate and fill it with one hand. "My reputation as a cretinous sporting man of no social graces will only be further confirmed."

"Nonsense," she said, putting a lobster patty on the plate for him. "You're the one who needs to be aided."

"But Cribb is thought to be better in both strength and technique than Hill," Iverley continued, going back to the subject of the fight. "The odds are very much in favor of Cribb."

"Nonetheless, I will bet for Hill," she said airily. "I am a firm believer that agility and wits can occasionally triumph over brute force." This was how things were supposed to be going. Light banter about things he was interested in, while he looked at her with an expression of respect and interest. The hours of studying the sporting news were worthwhile.

He sat down next to her with a smile. "Are your brothers putting a bet down for you?"

"Oh, no. What would be the fun of betting when I am not even allowed to go? And I must admit," she said with a wry smile, "I'm not *entirely* sure I would enjoy spending the day watching two men pummel each other."

His eyes narrowed in a speculative expression. Had she said too much? Perhaps she should have waxed more enthusiastic about pugilism. She took a large gulp of champagne to cover the self-conscious blush she felt heating her cheeks.

"We should have a private wager then," he said in a low voice.

Something in his tone made the champagne burn all the way down. She rallied. "What, you go to the mill and me stay at home? How do I know you won't misreport the outcome? I'm afraid my potential winnings would have to be tempting indeed." For some reason, her heart had begun pounding very hard. She struggled to maintain a neutral expression.

"Your poetry collection."

"What?"

"I won it, do you recall?"

"Ah, but you have no interest in poetry." She realized with shame that she had been hoping he would wager something entirely different.

"Pearls thrown to the swine," he agreed cheerfully. "But nonetheless, the entire collection is mine. Perhaps I shall use the volumes to prop up uneven table legs, or as a doorstop in the cellar."

"You wouldn't," she said, both laughing and horrified.

"It all depends on Hill," he reminded her, putting up his fists and ducking and dodging in front of her.

"I refuse to wager my books on something so stupid as pugilism," she exclaimed, too indignant to care if this did not fit with her new dashing personality. "I'll buy them back from you. You must at least allow me the opportunity to do that."

He pretended to think for a long moment, his fingers stroking his chin. "Perhaps a trade," he said at last.

"Very well," she said, before he could change his mind. "Give me my books, and I will never mock your horsemanship or your poor judgment in horseflesh as long as I live."

He thought for a moment with his eyes turned to the ceiling and then gravely shook his head. "Something"—he leaned slightly closer—"something that means more to you."

"Like what?" Merciful heavens, what had she gotten herself into? Her heart was beating furiously again, flooding nervous anticipation down into her fingertips. Somehow she couldn't seem to take her eyes off his mouth.

"Not jewelry or any other fripperies," he was saying slowly. "You don't seem to care a rap for female furbelows. Something else." He looked into her eyes, with an expression of deep concentration. "I would like something from you that isn't tangible like books or money. I want something much more dear."

She swallowed quickly and looked around. The party of young people had gone back to the ballroom. The two gentlemen continued their rhythmic snoring. They were alone. She and Iverley. Alone.

Her mouth seemed to have gone very dry. He was going to kiss her. She'd never kissed anyone in her life. What if she did it wrong and gave him a disgust of her? Then all the hunting and driving and card playing in the world would never catch his interest.

His voice was soft. She could almost feel his breath caress her cheek. "Yes, if Hill wins, you get your poetry books back. If Cribb wins . . ." He smiled slowly. His mouth was only inches from hers. "If Cribb wins you have to spend the next week amusing my sister."

"What?" She sat back, stunned.

"I want your time," he said with abominable innocence. "Caro is in town, and she's dead set on doing all those things you and I hate. Gossip and walks in the garden and sedate drives into town to buy three inches of ribbon to trim a bonnet. I know you'd much rather be riding hell for leather with the hounds, but that's the price you'll have to pay for losing." He grinned and chucked her under the chin.

She silently bellowed an extremely unladylike curse. She'd convinced him too well. He thought of her as nothing more than a hoydenish tomboy who would be chafed at the idea of spending time doing ladylike things. It would be a good joke to deprive rough, wild Georgie Palmer of the opportunity to hunt and shoot with the lads. He hadn't thought of kissing her any more than he'd thought of kissing his horse.

Georgiana wished for a moment that her dedicated studying of the art of pugilism had included more practicable techniques.

"Yes," she said with a weak attempt at laughter, "that's the price I pay."

Nine

The boxing match had been everything one could have hoped for. Hill showed enough skill to make things interesting, but not enough to challenge the near-deity status of Cribb. There was pushing and fighting enough in the crowd to delight the heart of any sportsman, and Richard had had the honor of a black eye from the judge himself. Strange that Iverley hadn't felt able to concentrate on it.

"Brilliant fun!" Richard exclaimed again, as they rode three abreast on the road home. "Did you see how he went down at the end? Right hook! Hill down like a sack of grain. I wish I'd bet more. I'd be rolling in the soft."

"All my winnings will go toward repairing my coat," William said ruefully as he examined the long tear down the seam of his jacket. "But at least I will be presentable at dinner. Mama will have fits over your eye, you know."

Richard poked at the rainbow-colored swelling around his brow bone and made a face. "Doesn't seem too bad. Perhaps she won't notice."

Iverley smiled into the clear autumn sky. Yes, it had been a perfect day. The turnup had been worth the ride, they had had good places in the crowds, and the man he'd backed had won. "Pity your sister couldn't be here."

The Palmer brothers both looked at him in surprise.

"Which sister?" asked William.

"Georgiana." It felt strange to say her name. He'd known it of course, but never said the word aloud. It was pretty.

"Ah yes. She would have loved it; particularly the part where Cribb cut his lip and blood went everywhere. Very artistic." Richard was laughing as though this were hilarious.

"Is she really so bloodthirsty?" he asked, surprised.

"Of course not," said William. "Richard is just attempting wit. Which he shouldn't do. I'm surprised to hear that you think Georgiana would have liked the bout. Ladies generally don't. But she has shown a new fondness for hunting lately. And she asked me to teach her to shoot."

"*I* was to have taught her to shoot," Richard objected. "But since you're a better shot, perhaps you'd better have a go at it. Of course you know she'll cry if she happens to hit anything."

"She has a cool head. She'll likely be a better shot than you," his brother said mildly.

Iverley wondered how they could be so careless of their sister's welfare. If Georgiana had been his sister . . . However, his conscience reminded him, he had never been overly protective of Caro. She would have spurned the chivalry of her younger brother.

But Georgiana was different. She seemed too delicate to be entering into such violent sports. She seemed strong, but breakable. He laughed such sentiments out of his head.

"She's not like most ladies," he said thoughtfully, interrupting a spirited discussion of boxing strategies.

"Who, Georgie?" asked Richard, as though he were surprised they were still on the subject of his sister. "I suppose she isn't."

"She's quite clever," William volunteered in his quiet manner. "Mama said she should hide it during her come-out. Which is ridiculous. I think it was a collection of rather dull-witted people who came up with the notion that men do not like an intelligent woman."

"I agree," said Iverley. "And it is so unusual to meet a woman with whom one shares so much in common."

Richard looked unimpressed. "I suppose. I mean, she's a great gun, but don't get any ideas that she's anything out of the common way. I mean, she is better than most, I suppose. Hard to say, when she's your sister."

"Exactly," William chimed in. "I would have said the exact same thing about *your* sister."

Iverley put his heels to his horse. Mention of Caroline reminded him that he had said he'd be back in time for dinner. "Perhaps that is all it is, then. Perhaps you always assume that your friends' sisters are different, because you end up knowing them better than most other women." He couldn't help but think privately that William and Richard did not appreciate Georgiana nearly enough.

"It is refreshing to meet a young lady who is so sincere," he continued after a moment. "So many women in London seem conniving. Always out to catch the richest man around. Always ready to use their wiles to get what they want."

"They aren't all like Miss St. James, you know," William reminded him.

He realized with a start that he hadn't thought about Muriel in a long time. How strange. At one point he'd actually entertained the notion that he would never get over her. "Of course they're not. And your sister proves it. She is the most genuine, unaffected, and honestly interesting woman I have ever met."

He felt rather foolish having said that, particularly in front of her brothers. He'd only meant it as a general compliment, but somehow it had come out sounding impassioned.

William and Richard exchanged a glance.

"Thought you were off the muslin company, Vaughn," Richard said with a sly wink.

"Oh, I am," he assured them with vigor. "Absolutely, off. Though," he added after they had ridden for a moment in silence, "she's quite the most fascinating female I've ever met."

"I think I hear the parson's mousetrap squeaking closed," Richard said with a dramatic flourish of his whip.

The elder Palmer brother joined in his laughter. "He can't hold out much longer. The Palmer charms are legendary."

"I meant it in the most general of ways," Iverley exclaimed, feeling unaccountably warm all of a sudden.

"Certainly," said Richard, "and you will be the most general of brother-in-laws."

"It's brothers-in-law," William corrected.

"No, it isn't. That sounds ridiculous."

"I'm right, I tell you. Brothers-in-law."

Iverley sat back and smiled. Their ridiculous raillery over Georgiana was forgotten in an instant, and he could admire her in private, since this looked to be the kind of argument that was likely to last all the way home.

* * *

Georgiana's shoulder was aching, but she trudged behind William along the ridge behind the stables. She'd been putting off the shooting lesson for weeks, but today her older brother, who was never one to renege on his promises, insisted that he fulfill his word that he would teach her.

Nonetheless, learning to shoot seemed unnecessary now. After all, she went out driving with Iverley and Richard nearly every day they weren't out hunting together. As her sportsmanship improved, she found that she could actually talk to Iverley without feeling quite so nervous.

Strangely enough, her plan seemed to be working. With so much in common, there was rarely a day she and Iverley didn't spend in each other's company. He sought her out for advice on horses and often came over for a hand of piquet after dinner in the evenings. Emily had slyly informed her last night that the gossips were saying they would be engaged by Christmas. Georgiana wondered why the thought twisted a knot of anxiety in her stomach.

"All right," William was saying cheerfully. "Now let's try a moving target." He scanned the trees and then gave a sharp order to his dog. The animal raced through the field before them, scaring up a brace of pheasants. Her brother raised the fowling piece up to his shoulder and giving a running commentary on his actions, neatly shot a bird out of the sky.

"There," he said, with an expression of satisfaction, "that's just how it should go. Do you think you can do it?"

"No."

William's good-natured face spread into an expression of encouragement. "Come on, Georgiana, of course you can. Where's the Dashing Georgie all the bloods in the county are in raptures over? They're all over themselves now that you've had this strange Corinthian start of yours." When she didn't respond, he gave her a rallying elbow in the ribs. "You did fine shooting at the target, once you got the hang of it."

"I know." She took the heavy gun from her shoulder and looked at it. "But I don't enjoy it." She offered the fowling piece back to her brother.

He looked surprised. "Ah now, you're just tired. I forget what it's like when you first start. Bruised are you? Well, to be honest you're a bit too small for a piece of that size. We'll try something different tomorrow."

"I don't want to do it again tomorrow. I have found that shooting is not something I want to learn after all." How could she explain to him that she was having second thoughts about the plan? Even though everything was going brilliantly, she found herself more and more often regretting its inception.

It seemed that the more time she spent with Iverley, the better the plan seemed to go. And the more convinced he became that she liked everything he did, the more like a fraud she felt. After all, where did it end? She couldn't very well keep up this pretense for the rest of her life. At some point she would have to admit she had pretended to be a sporting female just to entrap him.

"Oh come on. You'll enjoy it more once you're better at it," William prodded. "Besides, I thought you were quite keen to take it up. I didn't understand why, but you seemed dead set on it."

"I know, but I just can't. You're very kind to try to teach me, but I just don't care for it."

The dog had arrived back with the pheasant in his jaws, and set it down at William's feet, looking very pleased with itself. Will picked up the bird and patted the dog on its head. "Richard said something about how you were only on this sporting kick to impress Iverley." His calm eyes assessed her. "Is it true?"

Dear William, she could almost wish it were Richard who was confronting her. At least the younger of her two brothers seemed to understand to some degree her need to be someone Iverley could love. "I thought it would help if we had interests in common," she admitted.

"So you took up the sporting act on his account." His eyebrows rose. "Not wise, Georgiana. Your compatibility must arise from genuine common interests."

"I know," she said miserably. "But if I waited for that, he would never have spoken to me. He thought me missish and bookish. And so I have made an effort." She rubbed her shoulder and winced. "Oh, William, you are the only one I can say this to, but it is so very *tiring* being something I'm not."

He shot her an expression that, in a less kind person, might have indicated that he had told her so.

"And then, because I lost a bet with Iverley last week, I had to spend the day with his sister yesterday. I had the most wonderful time. We rode in the park and did not take any hedges at breakneck speed, and we talked about books, and the theater, and people we knew in common. . . ."

"And what is so terrible about that?"

She heaved a sigh. "It was terrible because it was lovely. Caroline is a very intelligent woman, and I enjoyed her company immensely. But it made me realize how much I enjoy doing those kinds of things, and how much I don't enjoy things like shooting."

"I don't understand what is so terrible about that.

No one expects you to become an expert shot or anything."

"Oh, but that isn't true. Iverley only condescends to speak to me because he thinks I'm interested in the same things as him. He detests women who care about literature and plays and things like that."

"I think," said William, "that it really isn't a question of *you* sharing interests with *him*. I think you would do better to consider if *he* shares anything in common with *you*."

Georgiana was silent for a long moment, considering this.

"Though," her brother continued, "I think you would do well to spend more time with Iverley's sister. Mrs. Markham seems like a very interesting and sensible woman."

"When did you meet her?" she asked in surprise.

He flushed slightly. "I danced with her at the Oldstones' ball." He suddenly bent down to examine something on the ground. "Oh look, the bishop head thistle. You don't see that commonly around here. I thought it was far too cold for it here. But we've had an uncommonly mild autumn. Perhaps we've had some spread of it to this region after all."

"You danced with her?" she interrupted, laughing. "You never dance!" She regarded him for a moment. "You like her, don't you?"

"I think her esteemable," he replied in a tone that did not invite further questions. "And I am certainly not going to go about doing things I hate to get her attention."

"Besides dancing," she shot back, grinning. Of course William had a point; she knew that. Should she really consider giving up her plan? After all, if something was meant to be, did one really have to go into training to make it happen?

She helped William collect the botanical specimen while he lectured voluminously on thistle anatomy and reproduction. Generally she would have reminded him that she had no interest in the topic, but he evidently had no wish to be teased about Caro Markham, and she herself needed the time to think about the points her brother had made regarding Iverley. What if he never learned to like poetry? What if she had to play the role of Dashing Georgie forever?

William continued his monologue all the way back to the house while she mused. Well, shooting was definitely out. She gratefully handed over her pouch and horn to the gameskeeper and followed William in the kitchen door.

"Will, I want to ask your advice—"

"A pheasant!" Cook exclaimed, running over to examine the bird. "Oh, do come show Betty, she'll be delighted with it. I'll have her hang it, and we'll have it next week." The woman dragged her brother off to be exulted over by the kitchen staff.

Georgiana looked after him, knowing already what her brother would advise her to do. He would likely tell her to be herself and trust that Iverley would come to admire her. If only she could believe that that would happen. She couldn't just sit and wait and hope that he would notice her. She couldn't risk him slipping away. Not when Fate intended him for her.

The butler entered the kitchen, looking well pleased. "Ah, Miss Palmer, you have returned. Lord Iverley is here to see you. He said he came only to leave a letter. Shall I tell him to leave it or will you see him after you have had the chance to change?"

The phrase struck her as rather funny. "No, Morrow,

I think I've changed enough for Lord Iverley. I'll go in to see him directly." Then, ignoring the dumbstruck look on the man's face, she strode past him toward the drawing room.

Iverley looked up at her as she entered the room. His face lit up in a pleased smile. In a moment, all her resolutions to confess her perfidy escaped from her like air from an ascending balloon. He looked at her with the expression she had seen when she had first met him. That look that made her believe that she was the only woman in the world.

"You're back," he said, holding out his hands to her. "Were you riding?"

"Out shooting with William," she said, suddenly conscious of her plain green pelisse and muddy half boots. "I'm so sorry to receive you like this. But I didn't want to make you wait."

He had not let go of her hands. The warm pressure of them made her legs feel suddenly soft as tallow. "I would rather see you like this, back from doing something you enjoy, than dressed up in a fine ball gown when you are miserable," he said.

Perhaps now was the time to admit all. Yes, she should tell him what she was really like and hope for the best. She steeled herself. "Actually, I do rather like balls and ball gowns. And," she continued doggedly, "I have discovered that I do not like shooting. I'm sorry."

He dropped her hands and looked at her in mild surprise. "Why are you apologizing to me?"

She didn't have a very good answer. A thousand thoughts whizzed through her head. She could explain the whole plan, but it would sound so ludicrous. "Morrow said that you had a letter?" she said instead.

He grinned. "I have two. One from my sister, thanking you for a marvelous afternoon and begging you and your sister to accompany us on an expedition to Farley Orchards next week, and the other from me."

"Oh?" She found that the room suddenly seemed rather too hot. "Why would you need to write me a letter?"

"Because"—he pinched her nose in the brotherly way she detested—"I wanted to make the official announcement that you are now the proud owner of a lovely set of poetry books."

"I thought I had to entertain your sister for a week," she said, rubbing her sore shoulder. Brotherly. For all her troubles, she had advanced no further in his feelings than brotherly. What a ridiculous plan it had been.

"Well," he said, reaching over and rubbing her shoulder as if it were the most natural thing in the world, "she was very entertained. Said she had rarely met a woman with whom she had so much in common. You completely charmed her."

She swallowed and tried to concentrate on what he was saying. His hand moved over her shoulder in the same easy circular motion she herself had used. But somehow it was not at all the same. Her muscles were trembling more than relaxing under the gentle, steady pressure of his hands.

Her courage boiled away in the heat of the desire that coursed through her. Dear heavens, in another moment, she would throw herself at him and demand that he kiss her.

Instead, his hand dropped easily to the pocket of his coat, and he drew out two letters sealed with red blobs of wax and the Iverley seal. She drew a deep breath to marshal her senses and conceal the look of bovine adoration she suspected she had been wearing.

"You are a woman of infinite talents," he continued,

as though the touch between them had been something entirely ordinary. "My sister and I are as unalike in our likes and dislikes as any two people can be, and yet we have both exclaimed numerous times how much you have in common with us. Truly your interests are varied." He smiled with an expression of open pleasure. "I don't know which of us likes you more."

She was a fraud, an actress, an entrapper, a liar. She should tell him this moment that the real Georgiana Palmer was not the dashing and outgoing sportswoman, but was the shy and bookish girl his sister had spent the afternoon with. She would ignore the look of admiration in the unclouded hazel eyes that looked down into hers, and she would tell him.

"So," she heard herself say in a cheerful voice, "are we going driving tomorrow?"

Ten

Iverley looked up as Georgiana descended the stairs. Was it possible to be so beautiful and not be aware of it? Any other woman with her vibrant blue eyes and dramatically dark hair would be primping and flirting to best advantage. She wore a dark amber driving costume that emphasized the curve of her breasts with a band of gold ribbon tied close under them. The heavy silk dropped straight down from the gold band, but somehow managed to hint at the narrow waist and hips beneath. Georgie seemed to be far more interested in hounds and horseflesh than in the effect she had been having on him these days.

"You're ready," he said as offhandedly as he could. "You can get rigged out quicker than any female I know."

She grinned at him and shrugged her shoulders in her familiar devil-may-care attitude. He wondered how shocked she would be if she knew the thoughts that ran through his mind more and more often these days. Likely she would only laugh. Not a romantic bone in her body, Georgie.

"You know," she was saying, "Mama would have fits if she ever knew we went on these driving expeditions alone. She's under the definite impression that Richard accompanies us."

"Ridiculous," he said, just as though he were not delighted that Richard had found other things to do. "It's only you and I. It's not as though—"

"Exactly." She dismissed the notion with a flick of her hand. "And we have a groom with us. But of course, if one didn't know better, it does look a bit scandalous." She slipped her gloved hand into the crook of his elbow and laughed up at him as she pulled him out the front door.

He allowed himself to be led down the steps. Did anyone know better? After all, they had been spending a good deal of time in each other's company. It wasn't likely that the fact had been missed by the sharp eyes of the country gossips. Oddly enough, he found that he didn't care. In fact, he rather enjoyed it. If it was acceptable to court someone in a stuffy little drawing room, why should one not go driving if one wished?

Besides, he reminded himself sternly, he wasn't courting Georgie. If she even half thought he was, she'd be off like a shot. After all, half the men in the county were throwing themselves at her, and she had shrugged them off with the firm but polite explanation that they didn't know her well enough to be proposing a lifelong alliance.

He looked at her profile as he helped her into the curricle. He knew her. He knew her better than anyone. He'd spent every moment they were together absorbing her details, and now he felt like he knew her as he knew himself. And they were so alike.

"It's immaterial anyway," she was saying. "Richard said he'd come with us tomorrow. Apparently the curate's daughter has thrown him over."

He realized Georgie was still talking about her

brother's abandoned plan to accompany them on their drives. "I'm sure he's inconsolable," he said, feeling slightly annoyed at the thought of Richard's return. He took his seat beside her, suddenly strangely aware of where his limbs were in proximity to hers. Did she notice that his breeches were nearly touching the russet folds of her driving costume?

"Oh utterly inconsolable," she said with a cheerful flourish of the whip that caught the thong over the leader's ear just as he'd taught her.

He leaned back as they started down the road. It was pleasant to allow her to drive. She didn't seem to mind if he conversed with her or remained silent and admired the scenery. Or whatever else he chose to admire.

The lane was a fiery tunnel of autumn colors, and the energetic team seemed to enjoy prancing through the swirls of leaves that blew beneath their hooves. Iverley drew a deep breath and found that he was very glad indeed that Richard had not accompanied them.

Georgiana launched into yesterday's conversation on carriage building where they'd left off, but Iverley wasn't in the mood to discuss the merits of the high-perch phaeton as opposed to its more ordinary cousin.

"So the curate's daughter threw him over," he mused, leaning back and tilting his hat over his eyes. "I never thought I would see the day when Richard didn't get what he wanted."

"Oh, I don't believe he's languishing," Georgiana replied, laughing. "He affects these grand passions occasionally, but I don't believe he's ready to fall in love."

"Ready?" he repeated with a cynicism he didn't much feel these days. "In my experience the wiser one gets the less likely one is to fall in love."

Georgiana's eyes narrowed in concentration as she negotiated the turn onto the Sleaford road. He watched her profile as she judged the distance of a plodding farm cart and neatly overtook it.

"Well done," he murmured. "Shall we go out to Biddling Wells? Too far do you think?"

"Not at all. The team is fresh." She was silent for a moment. "Were you in love with Miss St. James?"

The sudden question surprised him. His initial reaction was to brush her off with an offhanded comment. For some reason, he found he didn't wish to discuss his former fiancée with Georgiana. But he tipped the hat from over his eyes and watched the countryside roll by while he formulated his reply. "I don't know," he said at last, unsuccessful at reaching a better conclusion. "I suppose I thought I was. She'd money and breeding and beauty . . . I didn't mind her company." He laughed. "I suppose with a ringing endorsement like that, there is little wonder that she threw me over."

"I don't believe Miss St. James loved you or Lord whoever-it-was that she ended up marrying."

"Hepplewell," he supplied.

"I mean," she said, her eyes widening as she turned to him, "not to say you are not worthy of love . . . or . . . or anything like that. I only meant that if she loved you, she wouldn't have thrown you over."

"Do watch the road."

"I feel a bit sorry for her," she continued, waving at a group of workers engaged in gathering in the late hay. "Perhaps one day she'll meet the man she was meant for, and then she'll already be married. Just think of how sad that would be."

"The man she was meant for?" He snorted. "Give over, Georgie. I didn't have you pegged as the romantic type. People in our position can't afford to subscribe to some romantic notion conceived by poets that there is only one person out there who was meant for you."

The idea made him uncomfortable. He had been genuinely attached to Muriel. If she had not thrown him over, he would have placidly married her and gone about the rest of his life. There was nothing so dramatic as Fate involved. He supposed, if they'd given it any consideration, there had been a point where he and Muriel had thought they were meant for each other.

But here he was, hardly a month later struggling with lascivious thoughts about Georgiana. It was obvious that one's heart, if that was the relevant part of his anatomy in this instance, could not be trusted.

"Oh, but I am the romantic type," she said feelingly. "And I do believe in that poetic nonsense."

He waited a moment for her to burst into raucous laughter, but she did not. He wondered what she would think of him if she knew how quickly he had gotten over the lovely Miss St. James. And how easy he had found it to replace that woman in his affections. Georgiana would likely label him a shallow jackanapes who knew nothing about finer feelings.

Which he didn't, he reminded himself. Better to stick with gentlemen's sports—things he was already competent in.

"I could not bear the idea of marrying someone I didn't know for certain was the man meant for me," she continued.

He stared at her determined profile. He hadn't really given it a thought, but he'd supposed that when Georgiana married, which was nearly inevitable for a woman in her position, that she would marry someone like herself. Someone sporting and jolly. Far more in

the style of the jovial country squire than the languishing Byronic hero. Someone more like, well, him.

"What do you mean, 'meant for you'?" he demanded, sounding slightly more aggressive than he
had meant to.

She stared at him with an innocently surprised expression. "You know. Fated."

Fated. He didn't like that word. He wanted to grab
his life and wrestle what he wanted out of it, not wait
around and hope for the best. The idea that he could
love only once in his life and that he had wasted that
chance on the false charms of Miss St. James was a
lowering thought indeed.

"What if the man Destiny meant for you is in the
West Indies or Spain or somewhere," he said in a teasing voice.

She smiled faintly and adjusted the reins in her
hands. "I suppose he could be. And if he was, I would
wait for him." She was quiet and confident, as though
she knew the man already.

He tried to picture her country squire pining away
for her in the tropical heat of a West Indian sugar plan-
tation. He would be quite middle-aged and fat, with a
big laugh and dogs always at his heels. Probably the
type who would hate London and would refuse to take
her there for the Season. The kind of uneducated lout
who thought puns humorous and could eat mutton
every night for dinner and never grow tired of it. He
was beginning to hate the man.

"What if he was in the West Indies, and he died of
a fever and you never even met him," he said, suddenly
determined to prove her ridiculous theory wrong.

Her profile was serene, but there was a stubborn look
about her chin. "Then I suppose I wouldn't marry."

He made a noise of disbelief. "It comes of all that

poetry reading. Whenever I think you're sensible, I have to remind myself that the first time I met you, you were spouting some nonsense about poetry."

The chin went up a fraction. "Well, I don't see how you can go through life, calmly knowing that someday you'll marry someone you don't love. I know marriage means less for a man than for a woman, and that your life is less likely to be affected by whom you marry, but I don't see how you can say that the finer feelings don't mean anything to you. Besides," she grumbled, "that was the second time we met."

He was beginning to feel rather trapped in this conversation. He wasn't certain he'd ever been in love with Muriel or with anyone, and Georgie seemed to think him a lesser kind of animal for it.

He looked around him for inspiration. The trees lining the road were blazing with aggressive reds and oranges, and the wind was sharp and clean. The cloudless sky was a flat blue like the painted belly of a dish. Everything was strong and clear. It was normally how he liked England best, but today the countryside seemed altogether too brazen.

"Love is imagined," he said, feeling unaccountably bad-tempered all of a sudden. "At least, romantic love like you mean. There's passion and there's affection. Nothing else."

"Well," she replied a little stiffly, "I suppose there is no sense in debating it, since we shall never agree." She wore an expression of annoyance mingled with disappointment on her face.

Anger flared up within him. What should he care what Richard's little sister thought of him? He had no intention of writing odes to her eyebrows or serenading her beneath her window. If that was what love was, she was right, he knew nothing about it, and had no interest in learning. "Now you're pokering up just like a female," he said, mostly to annoy her.

"I am a female," she reminded him, entirely unnecessarily. "Why shouldn't I act like one?"

He wished they could go back to talking about curricle making. At least then, he didn't feel like he was disappointing her. "Oh don't be cross, Georgie," he said, in his best elder-brother voice. "It's just that most of the time you're being such a great harum-scarum tomboy that I forget."

"Yes," she said in a strange voice. "I know."

Eleven

They rode in silence the rest of the way to Biddling Wells. It was more of a spring than anything actually engineered into real wells. Apparently it had been a Roman spa, for there were still vestiges of stone bathing pools and the foundations of several other buildings associated with the baths. Obviously it had never attained that level of grandeur associated with Bath, and had certainly never gained any popularity as a watering hole since.

Georgiana politely asked her groom to walk the horses and climbed down from the curricle unassisted. Iverley thought for a moment that she might still be piqued, but she came around to his side and took his arm with a smile that was slightly forced, but much more like her usual self.

"Come now, I won't be a milksop, I promise. How is your ankle?"

It was entirely mended, but he feigned great pain just to amuse her. He grimaced and moaned as he always did whenever she showed concern over him, and she chided him for being a great baby. Despite the tension remaining from their quarrel, it was companionable walking this way, him pretending that he needed her assistance and her pretending that she believed he needed it. They were like the oldest of friends who had no need to explain things to one another. Like a couple that had been married for decades.

Prickles ran up his arms at this last analogy, particularly sharp since their last conversation had made it clear how inappropriate it was. He untwined his arm from hers, but she did not appear to notice.

"I came here with Mama and Emily years ago," she said, evidently trying to make conversation against the sudden awkwardness. "It was spring though, and the place was covered in wildflowers."

He looked around at the trees that hung low over the stone pools. In the spring, it would have had that kind of overblown beauty that was supposed to inspire one to rhyming couplets. He rather preferred the trees bare and the water in the pools black and unruffled.

The place had its own kind of beauty this time of year, understated and stark. He walked to the edge of the largest pool and looked down into the clear, deep water. At one end was what appeared to be the source of the spring. Tiny bubbles rose up from cracks in the rocks and wiggled their way to the surface, where they made ever-widening rings. The floating leaves at the edges of the pool bobbed and danced in the little waves.

"Is it a hot spring?" he asked.

Georgiana looked up from where she was examining a piece of paving stone that had once been painted with bright colors. "I don't know. We certainly didn't swim in it when I was here last." She walked over to stand beside him. "Well, look, I suppose it must be. You can see a bit of steam rising off the water." She pointed to where ghostly wisps of vapor were hovering over the surface. "Shall I pitch you in so you can find out?"

"Don't," he said, with more urgency than he had intended. "I do not swim." If she had been like any of his male friends, she would instantly have shoved him into the pool. Instead, she looked at him with a slight frown forming between her fine brows.

"A great sportsman like you didn't learn?" she asked, a slight tone of taunting in her voice.

"No," he said shortly. "I didn't." He wondered if she thought less of him. "I didn't grow up near the sea," he added, feeling as though he were making an excuse.

She moved away from him, winding her way across the grass that grew up through the cracks in the tiled floors of what must have been caldariums and changing rooms for the Roman citizens. "I could teach you of course," she said. "But that would hardly be appropriate. I'm sure Richard would."

He didn't find the idea appealing. Richard was a good enough fellow, but he wasn't the type one could confide a weakness to.

Georgiana had walked over to the other side of the pool where there were stone steps cut into the masonry. It was a strange trick of the sky on the water that made her eyes look an impossibly brilliant blue when she looked at him. "I know it's dreadful, but I can't resist the temptation to go put my toes in it."

"Georgiana, I—" He wanted to shout at her to be careful, but stifled himself, realizing that it would only make him look like an overly protective swain.

"I know, I know," she muttered. She began gingerly making her way down the mossy steps. He watched the silk train of her driving costume follow her, resistant for a moment, and then collapsing down each step. He felt the same pull.

"And you must swear you won't tell Mama. She'll

have an apoplexy if she hears I took off my stockings in front of a gentleman. But," she said sweetly as she leaned over and slipped off a shoe, "sometimes it is hard for me to recall that you are a male."

"Oh give over," he said, trying not to look at the deep pool below him as he followed her down the steps. "Don't be cross about that. I didn't mean that I don't think of you as a female. I just . . ." He fumbled for the idea. "I just get along with you better than any other woman I know."

She ignored that as she tentatively stuck out her toe and dipped it into the water. "Lovely," she said with approval. "Very warm." And then, with little regard for her russet-colored gown, she swept the train into her lap, sat down on the step, and put both feet in.

Her ankles were slender, and her white feet were narrow and well formed. He should probably avert his eyes, or better yet, insist that she dress herself and not behave like a complete hoyden, but he did not. There was still the tension left over from their argument, but it was easy to forget it in the pleasant warmth from the steaming water. She seemed supremely unconscious of his gaze. He gingerly sat down beside her on the step.

"Wouldn't you like to—Oh, I suppose you can't. We'd never get your boots back on. Oh well." She wiggled her toes, examining the distorting effect of the water. Then she sighed. "I get along with you, too, Iverley. And I'm flattered, highly flattered indeed, that you enjoy my company. But"—her eyes fastened on his—"there are many things about me you don't know."

There was something so serious in her gaze that he felt uncomfortable. Though the heat of their disagreement had cooled, there was a strange tightness in the stillness between them. He felt the urgent need to diffuse it by splashing her with water, teasing her . . . or kissing her. He wondered vaguely if she would drown him if he attempted it. "I hope you're not going to start making bizarre confessions," he said lightly.

"But, Iverley—"

"Because if there are things you think I'd rather not know, you're probably right."

"Iverley, I—"

"No," he said, putting a finger to her lips. "Let me continue to live in ignorance. If you smothered your infant brother, or set fire to the neighboring village, I'm happier not knowing."

Her mouth moved under his finger, setting off strings of fireworks down his nerves. "I'm not—"

Not what? There was nothing that Georgie was not.

"I'm not what you think," she finished flatly.

He rolled his eyes and gave her an elbow in the ribs. "How do you know what I think you are, chit?"

She smiled faintly, though there was still a disturbing seriousness in her eyes. "I don't. What do you think I am, Iverley?"

The tension between them was unbearable. Her lips were full and so very soft. In another moment he really would kiss her, and then they'd be in the suds. Richard's madcap sister. It made no sense at all. How could he, the man who had sworn off women forever, in the space of a month come to the point where he desperately wished to kiss one? And her of all people. She was far more likely to pummel him than kiss him back.

Fated, a voice sang tauntingly in his head.

She was still looking up at him expectantly, her mouth mere inches from his own. He wouldn't do it. He wouldn't let control of his life be wrested from him by desire. Or attraction. Or Fate.

He struggled out of the grip of the moment and reached out and splashed her with the warm, sulfurous water. "I think you're going to catch the ague if you sit here with your feet in a pool of water in the middle of October. Come on, I'll drive back, and you can see how it's really done."

He thought for a moment that she was cross about the dark spots of water that now decorated her gown, but she didn't seem to notice them. Her expression was unreadable, but after a pause, she nodded, got to her feet, and began pulling on her stockings. Unable to withstand the temptation of her pretty white calves, he turned and fled up the stairs.

Twelve

He did not come to see her the next day. Or the next. Or the day after that.

He hadn't seemed angry when they parted on that day they drove to Biddling Wells, but he didn't come to drive with her again. Perhaps her talk of love and destiny had given him such a disgust of her that he didn't wish for her company. Or was the shock of her disagreeing with him, for the first time in their acquaintance, too much for his delicate sensibilities? Or perhaps her awkward preliminary advances toward a confession had hinted at too much. Maybe he already knew her shameful secret, and he had taken himself off.

It didn't matter why though. He still didn't come. She wouldn't have to confess at all then, she reminded herself as she closed the pianoforte and gathered together her music. It was for the best that he didn't.

"Where is Lord Iverley?" Emily asked, putting down her sewing and looking at the clock on the drawing room mantel. "Why don't you go driving together anymore?"

"It looks a bit wet out," Georgiana replied, drawing aside the curtain to pretend she was looking at the sky instead of down the empty road. "Besides, I think everyone is at some race meet."

Emily looked sly. "You had a tiff, didn't you?"

"Not at all."

It wasn't a tiff; it was the sad, quiet realization that there were unbreachable differences in their characters.

Her sister examined her stitches, then sighed and began to pick them out. "It seemed like things were going extraordinarily well. He came to drive with you every day, and I know very well that Richard didn't accompany you most of the time. If he hasn't kissed you by now, I shall think you a very poor-spirited creature indeed." Her eyes opened wider. "Is that what the tiff was about?"

"No." Unfortunately.

A sense of loss tore deeply into her. It was for the best, she reminded herself again. If he no longer wished to see her, she would not have to admit that she'd gone to so much effort to catch his notice.

She looked down at the sporting papers scattered on the drawing room table. And she wouldn't need to bother with those any longer.

Fate had obviously made a terrible mistake. Iverley was nothing like what she'd made him out to be. He did not believe in love. There was passion and affection, he had said, nothing else. At most she had aroused a brotherly affection in him, certainly not passion. And even that affection was due to her grand deception.

She waved her hand in a gesture meant to be dismissive. "I've gone off Iverley. It was too much trouble. I was making myself out to be someone I'm not. That is to say, I have grown to enjoy hunting and driving. And there are aspects of pugilism and horse racing I suppose I have come to appreciate, but I have come to realize that there are things in life I enjoy much more."

"But Iverley was just beginning to like you," Emily protested innocently. "Before, he thought you a complete featherwit."

Georgiana wished sometimes that her sister did not have quite so perfect a memory. "But what is the use of him liking me when it was not really *me* that he liked? I never should have embarked on it. If you are meant to be with someone, you should not have to change to make them admire you."

She was changed though. Her first feelings for Iverley had been of infatuation. But over the months she had grown to know him so much better. And he proved so much more than merely a man who had looked at her with Fate in his eyes. And as her feelings deepened from infatuation to love, she had slowly, painfully grown to realize that she could never have him.

The very scheme that was to have won him was what would drive him away. If she admitted it, he would be repelled by her machinations. If she did not, she would continue to lie to the man she admired most in the world.

And worst of all, the more of herself that she showed to him, the less he liked her. His expression, when she tried to explain what love meant to her, was nothing but scornful. And now, after one glimpse at her soul, he didn't wish to see her at all.

Yes, Fate was giving her a rather painful learning experience.

"Oh dear." Emily sucked the end of a thread and then squinted at her sister through the eye of her needle as she threaded it. "Is Lord Perfect not so perfect after all?"

Georgiana sighed. "I suppose it was inevitable. He

is a man with many admirable qualities. It was shallow of me to have judged him perfect before I really knew him. And he *is* perfect." She shrugged. "Just not perfect for me."

"Ah well," said Emily with a shrug of her own. "There's always Cousin Elliot."

Georgiana could not help but laugh. "No, I won't marry him either. But don't worry. You'll have your Season next spring. I shall graciously step down to allow you to have the stage."

Her sister leaned back on the couch and struck a dramatic pose worthy of Mrs. Siddons. "And I suppose you'll go into a decline and be driven to a loveless early grave?"

Georgiana twitched the curtains closed with a gesture of finality. "Of course not. I only meant that my idea was foolish, and I am tired of pretending to be something I'm not. Lord Iverley and I were mismatched from the first. Now, shall we go for a quick walk in the garden? There is a bit more light before dinner and the rain has held off."

From now on she would stop pretending. She had been foolish to think she could wring love from a stone. In a way she was relieved. No more pretending to be interested in Mendoza's left hook or whether Smithfield's bay was narrow in the chest.

And in a way she was miserable.

There was the sound of someone noisily ascending the stairs and Mrs. Palmer burst into her room. "Drat that boy!" she exclaimed. "Inviting people to dinner when he knew good and well that Cook had nothing prepared but grouse and that ham we've been eating for weeks."

"What boy?" Georgiana asked.

"Your brother Richard," she replied, giving her

daughter a look of annoyance that suggested Georgiana was entirely responsible for the relationship. "Apparently we are having a dinner party. Not that I am ever consulted about these things. He has invited over half the sportsmen in the county without asking me."

"I'm certain he only invited them because he knows that you are the best hostess around," she said soothingly. "Everyone says so. He's dreadfully proud of it."

Mrs. Palmer looked somewhat mollified. "Well, I don't see how he expects us to go conjuring up something from nothing but grouse and ham. Do be a dear and entertain everyone until I change. And don't let Emily start showing off." She shot a warning look at her youngest child. "She will dominate the conversation entirely, you know." She threw up her hands and bustled out of the room.

There was every likelihood that Iverley would be downstairs. How would he act? Was he still angry? She reminded herself that it didn't matter anymore how Iverley felt. Very well, she *hoped* she would see him. Tonight would be a new beginning. Tonight she would start acting like herself again.

Her eye caught the sporting newspapers lying on the drawing room table. They were underlined, circled, and annotated like a scholar's textbook. With a strange sense of freedom, she gathered them up and put them in the fire. For a moment they lay there smoking, then they shriveled a little, curled at the edges, and burst abruptly into flames. "Come on, Emily," she said shortly, "let's go downstairs."

Thirteen

Richard rushed over when Georgiana entered the drawing room. "I say, Mama is just as mad as fire isn't she? Well it isn't all my fault. I told William to tell her but somewhere along the way the message got lost. It's just we were having such a grand time that I thought it would be great fun to continue the party here. Much nicer than the inn, and you know Mama's cook is top notch."

"She'll come around," Georgiana assured him. Despite her promise to herself, she found herself scanning the room. She recognized several of the faces as particular friends of Richard's.

Caroline was there, standing with William and Mr. Hennings. Georgiana felt pleased, but at the same time wary. If Caro was invited, then Iverley must be, too. At last she saw him, standing at the mantel looking intently into the fire. He looked at her and gave her a tight smile, but did not cross the room to her. For the first time, it truly dawned on her that everything between them had changed. It wasn't an easily explained mistake. Somehow, between that day at the wells and now, everything had changed.

"Will," she said, ignoring the strange tightness in her chest as she crossed the room to him. "Mama will be down in a moment. I hope you have won enough money at the races to be able to buy her a very nice present for descending upon her like this."

"Poor Mama." He grinned, looking very like Richard for a moment. "We're quite a trial to her. But she will rise to the occasion. She always does."

"Have we surprised her?" asked Caro. "Mr. Palmer made it sound as though we were expected. I hope we aren't an inconvenience."

"I was the one who didn't relay the message, I'm afraid," William said sheepishly.

"Don't worry at all," Georgiana assured her, forcing a laugh that sounded too explosive. "Mama prides herself on being able to entertain at a moment's notice. She actually loves a little flurry. I expect the gentlemen will have to sustain the indignity of there not being enough ladies, but I suspect a little of Mama's lemon cake and a sample of my late father's superior port will go a long way to make up for that lack."

Mr. Hennings laughed. "Your sister has already assured us that she must have a man for each arm as she is led in to dinner."

Georgiana threw a glance over to where Emily was shouting with laughter in the center of a group of her brother's friends. "I should think it would take two to restrain her, yes."

"Your brother tells me you have taken up driving."

"A bit," she said, resisting the urge to look at Iverley. No. From now on she would be plain Miss Georgiana Palmer. Dashing Georgie was gone forever. "But I am particularly fond of poetry."

Hennings looked mildly surprised at the aggressive tone of this announcement. "What type of poetry in particular, Miss Palmer?"

In explaining her taste in literature, she found that

Hennings was pleasingly well informed, and they enjoyed a conversation on the subject that lasted until the time came to go in to dinner. When she quite naturally accepted his invitation to escort her into the dining room, she saw with surprise that Iverley was staring at her from across the room with an expression of strong disapproval.

To her discomfort, she found that she was seated between the two of them. Iverley allowed Hennings to settle her in her chair and sat stiff and silent without attempting to engage her attention. When the second course came, she turned to him, but he merely continued to eat, apparently listening to the conversation about the race meet that was going on across the table. When she wasn't hiding behind her character of the harum-scarum Georgie, she found that she had little idea of how to start a conversation with him.

At last, when the covers were being removed, she turned to him again. "I'm delighted you brought your sister to dinner, Lord Iverley," she said. It seemed that a fondness for Caroline was the only thing they had in common these days.

"Your brother William invited her," he said shortly. Then, after a pause, "She is to drive into Lincoln on Wednesday and mentioned that you might wish to join her. I am certain that she will ask you."

"I would enjoy that," she replied. She cleared her throat. "I enjoy going visiting and having a comfortable coze with a friend." She wanted to go on and announce that she liked sewing and writing letters and talking about news and people as well, but it somehow didn't seem to fit into the conversation.

"Gossip, you mean." His dark brows rose in an expression of mild contempt.

"Certainly," she said with an overbright smile, stretching it until it hurt.

"Or flirting?" There was a sharp note in his voice.

Emily, the center of attention, had plucked a rose from the centerpiece and was replacing the bloom in Mr. Jenner's buttonhole. Georgiana rolled her eyes. "You mustn't criticize my sister. She is not yet out and is just testing her wings."

Iverley turned back to his plate. "I didn't mean your sister," he said darkly.

Georgiana would have liked to ask him exactly what he did mean, but at that moment her mother rose and announced loudly that the ladies would withdraw.

She followed them up the stairs, listening to her mother scold Emily. Why had Iverley been so annoyed? Resolved to show her true self from now on, she expected him to be surprised, disappointed, and then quickly to lose interest in her. Instead he seemed angry.

It didn't matter that she didn't understand him, she reminded herself. There was no reason she needed to do so. He was not perfect. And it was not Fated. She sat down at the seat of the pianoforte and began to play.

She would miss him though, a small part of her admitted. It would be a relief to stop having to pretend enthusiasm for things she didn't care for, but she would certainly miss the time they spent together. She thought of the way he used to laugh and tease her as he instructed her in driving, and how, despite his declarations of impatience, he did everything possible to please his sister.

"Oh, do stop playing such a melancholy air. Play something jolly," Emily insisted. "Mama, do you think we could have dancing?"

"Absolutely not!" her mother exclaimed. "Emily, you have gone stark wild. Unless you want everyone to think you a perfect hoyden when you make your bow next Season, you must behave with more refinement."

"Are you quite all right?" Caroline asked quietly at her side.

"Certainly," she said with a good deal too much cheer. "Why should I not be?"

"You've played that piece three times over." Caro's brows rose slightly in an expression of pointed inquiry. She looked very like her brother for a moment.

Georgiana dropped her hands to her lap. "Likely because I don't know any other pieces. I love music, but hate to practice." She decided to turn the topic away from herself as quickly as possible. Caro was too observant by half. "I saw that William was telling you about the botany book he is writing. I must apologize. He is as mad for plants as my father was for birds."

To her surprise, Caroline blushed pink. "No, I didn't mind. I found it rather interesting. In fact"—she shuffled through the music at the instrument as though she were looking for something—"I said that I would go with him on his next expedition to look for specimens. That is, if you are going," she added quickly.

Caro and William? That was an interesting thought. She'd never really considered the possibility of someone conceiving a *tendre* for her brother. They were well matched, though. Serious and intelligent, they had compatible temperaments, and apparently many common interests as well. Neither one of them was putting on a masquerade, in any case, she thought with guilt.

"Certainly," she replied. "William knows everything that grows in the whole county. He's found quite a few interesting specimens here that are quite different from what is found elsewhere."

Iverley's sister set the disordered sheaf of music back on the pianoforte. "Yes, he's really quite clever. I mean, when it comes to botany. That is, most people don't know anything about botany—" she trailed off, looking flustered.

Georgiana raised an eyebrow and went back to playing the same dirgical song.

"Dear Mrs. Markham, do come look at my latest bird drawings," Mrs. Palmer called from across the room. "Emily says the swallow looks more like a flying currant bun, but I must disagree."

Poor Caro was mediating a spirited debate on the characteristics of flying baked goods when the gentlemen entered.

"Miss Palmer," said Mr. Barrow, "we must call upon you to settle a question between Hennings and myself."

"I should hardly think I am qualified." She laughed, continuing to play the pianoforte.

"Ah but you are," said Mr. Hennings. "I maintain that girls should be taught Latin, the same as boys so that we should all be made to suffer equally. Mr. Barrow says, instead, that neither should be taught it, and that all Latin teachers should be burned at the stake."

Iverley had crossed the room and was examining the pictures on the walls. He still looked out of temper. Good heavens, would this dreadful night never end?

"Well," she said with a smile that felt forced, "I agree with you both."

"You can't," they both protested. "We've ten pounds riding on your answer."

"But at the root of your question you do not disagree. You both think that boys and girls should be taught equally. And I think that everyone should be taught following his or her own inclination and ability."

"Ha!" said Barrow. "And no one has either inclination or ability to learn Latin."

"I rather liked it," she murmured. Iverley had now turned on his heel and was bearing down upon them with a frown like a thundercloud.

"Ha!" countered Hennings. "She has been taught Latin and she enjoys it. I rest my case."

"Miss Palmer," Iverley said gruffly, "might I have the honor of a turn about the room?"

"I'm in the middle of a piece," she reminded him, continuing to play.

"Your sister can play. Or God forbid, we can go a moment without some infernal instrument going." His mouth was a straight white line. "I have an interest in one of those pictures over there." He made a jerky gesture toward the other side of the room. "And I hoped you could answer my questions."

"Ah," she said, smiling at Hennings and Barrow, "an emergency indeed. I hope you will excuse me." She rose and walked with deliberate slowness across the room. "What was it you wished to know?" Her tone was cheerful. "Or did you merely mean to embarrass me?"

"Embarrass you?" he countered, his voice low and dangerous. "Keep you from making a fool of yourself, more like. What do you think you're about, flirting like that?"

"Flirting?" She almost laughed aloud. "Me?" The only man she'd ever flirted with in her life was him.

"If you have little enough care for your own reputation, I would think you should care about your brothers'. They would surely not want it bandied about that their sister is an incorrigible hoyden."

Georgiana looked over to where Richard and William were pulling chairs up to the card table. "They do not seem overly concerned with my behavior." She gave him a thin smile. "I do not see why you should be."

"You are determined to vex me." He looked for a moment as though he would like to shake her. "I know you to be a sensible woman. A woman with no featherwit affectation, no missish ways. And yet all evening you've done nothing but laugh and flirt, and talk of music and poetry and fashion and people, just like some . . . some"—he searched for the word—"some ordinary girl."

She drew herself up to her full height and looked him in the eyes. "I am an ordinary girl," she said with extreme deliberateness. "And I'm afraid you don't know me at all."

Fourteen

Iverley tipped his hat lower over his eyes and slouched down in the carriage seat. After two weeks of the same, it was merely another ridiculous evening to be spent bowing over people's hands, dancing country dances, and eating the inevitable lobster patties. One would think that after the Season in London, the last thing people would wish to do would be to entertain, but somehow life in the country became just another round of social gatherings.

"I declare, Iverley, you haven't been listening to a word I've said," Caroline scolded.

"No," he agreed.

"But it is said to be marvelous. Quite puts Vauxhall in the shade. I love water gardens, and Thomlinson appears to be obsessed with them. They say the fountains circulate thousands of gallons of water an hour. I wonder how one measures that. Of course, it really is too cold for an outdoor party, but I daresay we can walk in the gardens briefly and then go in to warm ourselves up."

Iverley grunted.

"Good heavens but you've been a bear of late," his sister continued. "What ever has happened to put you so out of temper?"

"I'm not out of temper," he snapped. Why should he be? This was the autumn of celebrating his new-found bachelorhood. He could do anything he liked, with no thought to what anyone else wanted. Except that Caro kept dragging him to these dashed balls. Why should she need him for an escort anyway? She could have Georgiana go with her if she wished for company. After all, the two were bosom bows these days. Neither had any need for him. A day didn't go by when they weren't out walking or driving together. Ever since that day at Biddling Wells, Georgiana had seemed transformed into a completely different person.

"I do hope you'll dance with Georgiana," Caroline said, as though her thoughts had turned in that direction, too.

"Why?" he demanded, ungraciously.

"Why indeed! Because she's the sister of your best friend, and a dear friend of mine. Because she always praises you to the skies."

He sat up slightly straighter. "Does she?"

"She tells everyone you taught her to drive. And she says you're a fine sportsman."

That was all? "Why doesn't she hunt anymore?" He had gone down to every meet, thinking he would see the familiar gray habit and that ridiculous cap with the red feather, but she never appeared.

"She does, only she rides over to Lord Hudsbeth's meet in Reedham. She says his men draw better than Henning's. Or something like that. I don't really know what she's talking about when she goes on about hunting."

"Oh." He slouched back down again and took a deep interest in settling the cuffs of his coat. "I have hardly seen her in weeks. I suppose she is doing well."

"Certainly. Why shouldn't she be? Why just the other afternoon she was telling me that she was hoping to go to visit her aunt and uncle next spring in Scotland. Of course it would mean that she would miss the Season, which would truly be too bad. However, it is her little sister's turn to come out this time, so I don't know if she would have been able to go to London, in any case. I don't think Georgiana really cares that much about going about in society though, so she'd likely enjoy Scotland far better.

"Perhaps she will fall in love with a nice Scotsman," Caroline continued. "That would be nice, don't you think? Though then we should never see her, which would be dreadful. Perhaps the Scotsman can be prevailed upon to move in this direction. If he truly loved her, he would, wouldn't he?"

"You're nattering, Caro." He turned his attention out the coach window again. What was it about Georgiana that he couldn't stop thinking about her? It wasn't that he missed their heated debates on boxing matches, though she was well informed. And of course he could go hunting and driving with any number of people. There was nothing he did with Georgie that he couldn't do with other people, but somehow it was not the same. It was solely and wholly her company that he missed.

It was his own fault. He'd realized at Biddling Wells that something special had grown up between them. For all his claiming to himself that she was a friend like any of his male friends, his feelings for Georgie were very different. For God's sake, he'd nearly kissed her! For the sake of his own sanity, he'd put some space between them after that. He shouldn't be surprised she'd found other things to do. And other people to do them with.

At last the carriage pulled up in front of the Tomlinsons' country house. Two large fountains sprayed a fine mist into the air on either side of the door. Caro's enthusiastic admiration was cut short when she realized her silk wrap was being spotted with water, so she pulled him inside. The entrance hall was drier, but no less opulent. His sister cooed in approval, but he couldn't wait to discard his great coat and slink off in search of the card room. It was merely another evening of stupefying boredom, trapped in a room, however grand, full of the same people one saw every week.

After the necessary polite conversation with their hosts, he made his escape. It was early, and the card room was nearly empty. Georgie was likely walking in the water gardens like most of the other guests. He sat down in a chair and took a glass from the waiter. Even the champagne tasted flat. He quelled the urge to go search the house for her. She had a right to do anything she liked, and there was no need for him to go puppying after her, if she had no desire to see him.

Perhaps he should go back to London. Surely the news of his broken engagement would have died down by now. There would be little to do there this time of year, but there would be more variety in the insipid entertainment than here.

"There you are, Iverley," Richard said, popping his head in the doorway. "I say, have you seen the water gardens? Funniest thing I ever saw. Tomlinson's quite cracked you know. Some of the fountains are quite nice. Most of them are in the common way, anyway. Then there's all kinds of things he's invented himself. Water leaping all over the place. Tunnels and walls, all made of water. Even a thing that when you walk down it, your steps set off some mechanism that makes water burp up across the lawn in different patterns in the most hilarious way." He seated himself next to Iverley and shuffled the pack of cards in front of him. "I quite doused Lady Heathercock. She was mad as fire."

"You should go have a look," Richard continued when he did not respond. "The ladies were all prepared to be in raptures about them, but a good half of them have gotten splashed in some way or another, so they aren't nearly so keen. And poor Tomlinson nattering on about the architecture of water and liquid sculptures."

Iverley felt a prickling at the back of his neck and stifled the urge to turn around in his chair.

"Come now," Lord Exeter was saying, "do let's play that game again. The one you made up at the Hudsbeths' party."

"Where each of the card numbers stand for a different letter, and we have to make sentences," Hennings provided.

Iverley had never realized what an irritating voice Hennings had. He clenched his jaw and pretended not to see them.

"No," Georgie replied, "I don't believe I wish to play after all."

"Then perhaps you wish to dance?" Exeter suggested, with the most ludicrous note of hopefulness in his voice.

"Would you mind terribly if I did not?" she asked. Iverley thought she sounded tired, but perhaps it was only his imagination. The desire to turn and look at her pulled at him, but he resisted. What would he do if he saw her? Say hello? Plunge into some vapid, meaningless conversation about how marvelous everything was? They hadn't conversed in weeks, and it seemed like every ability to do so had dried up between them. He pretended intense concentration on the hand of cards Richard had dealt him.

"Lord Exeter," said Hennings, "perhaps you would procure Miss Palmer a glass of orgeat."

Georgiana demurred, but Hennings insisted. "While you are drinking it, you can make up your mind about what you would like to do."

Exeter passed Iverley's table with a sulky expression on his face. Iverley scowled in return. He should be glad that he himself was not one of the swains dancing attendance on Georgie. What a fool he must have looked weeks ago when he was living in her pocket. He strained to hear, but the voices behind him sank to a low murmur.

"Piquet!" Richard exclaimed. "I say, my luck's in tonight. Generally you beat me every time. Losing your touch, my friend."

Iverley resisted the urge to shush him, but the voices behind him dropped even lower.

"I can't," he heard Georgiana say at last. "Not on my own. Perhaps Emily would like to come."

"Let's find her," Hennings agreed. "Though very likely she's out there already. I admire your sense of propriety, but we will hardly be alone there, you know."

He heard chairs scrape the floor and the rustle of her gown as they left the room. Only at the last moment did he raise his eyes to see her leave. She wore silver, trimmed with gray. It made her dark hair appear nearly black and her skin a flawless white. The effect was starlike, luminous. Ridiculous, milksop similes flooded his head. Good God, in another moment he would be composing limp poetry in her honor.

Then the door closed behind her, the hairs at the

back of his neck lay down, and the room was again full of the ordinary hubbub of card play.

He continued to lay down cards mechanically for a few moments, barely listening to Richard's continuous commentary.

"I daresay it will be good to have Georgiana marry," Richard was saying cheerfully. "Though I must say, it will be a sight more of a relief to get Emily fired off. The girl's more trouble than a monkey. Georgie's turned down loads of offers before, but she's been different lately. Thoughtful-like. I think she's ready to settle now."

"Georgie? Marry?" A horrible notion struck him. Hennings. Of course. The puppy fancied himself in love and was going to propose. Tonight. In the gardens. In two minutes Emily would have scampered off somewhere and the two of them would be alone. Perhaps even right now, she was—

"Bizarre, isn't it? Especially when she's been so harum-scarum of late." Richard chewed his lip and squinted at his cards for a moment. "She's had three offers once she started playing the dashing sportswoman. Turned them all down, though. I suppose I don't blame her. I wouldn't want to marry Quigley either, but Mama's been impatient—"

Iverley didn't hear him. His chair skidded back as he stood abruptly.

"Where are you going?" Richard demanded. "We're in the middle of a hand!"

He strode out of the room, only vaguely aware of the interested murmur of conversation that followed him. Pushing past the damp and querulous party coming in through the back doors, he suddenly found himself breathless with the shock of the cool night air.

The scene itself was enough to take one's breath

away. The entire length and breath of the garden as far as the eye could see was sparkling with water. It shot from jets, sprayed from fountains, and flowed down channels. Nearer the house were more conventional basins with the contorted shapes of river gods and mermaids spewing mist into the air. Further in, he saw tranquil pools reflecting the light of the lamps that lit the garden from elaborate iron lampposts. The crowds took little notice of the scene as they wrapped their dripping cloaks around them and hurried back toward the house.

There was no sign of Georgie or Hennings.

Surely the man would have picked a romantic place to propose. Iverley looked around; there were too many choices. Beside the marble channel where water slid smooth as glass? In the grove where jets sprayed the shimmering shapes of trees into the air?

The garden was almost empty, and now he saw why. The water seemed to leech away any last warmth of the day. He shoved his fists into the crooks of his elbows and ignored the cold. Perhaps he had been wrong. Perhaps Hennings was even now proposing to Georgiana in a cozy little salon or in a corner behind a potted palm. He marched faster down the wet paving stones.

A stream of water burst up beside him, and he suppressed a yelp of surprise. Another step and water shot up and arched in a shiny stream over the walkway itself. He noticed that it was a black paving stone that triggered the fountains' mechanism. He found the next stone and sprayers began turning a little pinwheel round and round.

"Mad," he muttered, in no mood to admire Lord Tomlinson's whimsical creations. He quickened his pace, trying to avoid the black stones. What if even now she had said yes and was in his arms? He gave up avoiding the foot mechanisms and strode faster, ignoring where his feet fell. Water leapt and sprayed in a frenetic dance around him. He turned to his left, noting with grudging admiration that the last trigger made a stone cannon shoot an enormous bolus of water at the side of a stone ship that promptly sank into a miniature harbor.

Where was she? His insides gave a jerk when he saw Emily, alone, dancing about and laughing with glee as jets of water leapt up around her.

"Where is she?"

"Oh, Lord Iverley! Isn't this brilliant? See, there's a pattern. First one goes off there, then all the ones on the outside, then, oops! I should have told you to move. Then the one to your left, and then, oh dear, we'd better run, because then they all come on at once." She pulled him out of the way just as a dozen spouts turned on. The water sprang up into the air and seemed to hang there for a moment in wobbling globes before it fell back to the ground with a splat.

"Where is your sister?" he demanded urgently.

"Oh, she walked off with Hennings a moment ago." Emily laid a finger beside her nose and gave a broad wink. "I expect he had something of a private nature to ask her."

"Where?"

Emily pointed to a fountain that sprayed fans of mist in a long row. "Why do you wish to stop them? Is there something wrong with Hennings? Is he Not At All What He Appears To Be?" Her voice rose as Iverley strode away. "A Villain? A Rogue? A Murderer?"

A sense of foolishness overwhelmed him. Emily had a point. Why did he wish to stop them? If he came upon them embracing, what exactly did he think he would do? He wished for a moment that Hennings did have some hideous past, but he knew the man well, and unless imperfect table manners and an overwhelming need to visit his mother every week could be counted as crimes, there was no reason to interrupt their bliss.

He rounded the fountain with a sense of dread, but there was no one there. The breath hissed out of him. A voice in his head said with irritating rationality that he should go back to the warmth of the house, have a drink, and thrash Richard at piquet.

Then he saw her. She was sitting so still that at first, in the frenzy of water that danced everywhere, she was nearly invisible. She was alone, her silver gown seeming to give off its own light in the dimness. He walked over to the bench where she sat at the foot of a wall of water. She was facing it, her head bowed down, as though she had fallen asleep sitting up.

Her dark hair was dressed high on her head with two long curls escaping on the left side. The back of her neck looked vulnerable and exposed. He had the strange urge to kiss her there. He beat back that wild notion, uncomfortable with its strength.

Just when he thought perhaps she truly was asleep, she turned her head and looked at him.

Her eyes shone dark in the torchlight, her lashes casting long shadows across her cheeks. "Iverley," she said in a tired voice, as though his appearance were the last thing she needed.

He seated himself beside her, not caring if she wanted him there or not. "What happened?"

"Nothing." She sat with her gaze fixed on the water that flowed a silky black down dark granite veined with gold.

"Where is Hennings?" The feeling of foolishness was creeping over him again.

"I asked him to go." She turned and looked at him for a moment, her lips thin and white with suppressed emotion. "I think you should go too."

He sat where he was, listening to the water chatter softly to itself as it slid to the bottom of the wall.

"Go!" she exclaimed with more force, when he did not move. "I wish to be alone. We have not spoken for weeks and then you come bumbling in at a private moment and want to talk."

There was something rather endearing about the way her brows drew together when she was angry. He suppressed the urge to reach out and smooth them.

"You're impossible," she continued. "I disagreed with you about one thing weeks ago, and you ceased speaking to me. Do you cut off all your friends if they counter you?"

Did she really think that? That he'd been avoiding her because of their disagreement? How could he explain that it was something quite the opposite of dislike that had forced him to take some time to get his emotions under control.

"Fate," she said, evidently mistaking his silence for confusion. "We argued about Fate." In the flickering dimness he could see spots of color appear on her cheeks. "And why should it have mattered that we disagreed?" she went on. "How could it possibly matter that you don't believe that one person is Fated to be your one true love. You and I were merely friends."

Merely friends? But surely she felt the pull between them. Surely she, too, experienced that strange, futile struggle against desire when they were close. Was it possible that he'd allowed the incredible similarity between them to fool him into thinking there could be something more?

Her voice had risen higher as she grew impassioned in this one-sided debate. "And now we are not even friends."

The silence was louder than her voice. Far away he heard the shrill feminine squeals of guests doubtless being doused with water.

They could go back to being friends. It could be just like it was. They could go riding and driving and spend their time talking of the sporting news just as they used to. But he knew now that friendship with Georgiana Palmer would never be enough.

Fifteen

She felt like a fool ranting on to him about friendship and Fate. He couldn't know how painful it was for her to see him again. She'd made her resolution though, and she'd stick with it. She would not go back to acting like the old Georgie he knew, just to make him like her.

He sat calmly but his expression was tight, almost angry. "Georgie," he said at last, waiting until she looked up at him to be certain he had her full attention. "You can't marry Hennings."

Her back straightened. "And why not?" Of course the obvious reason why not was because she had told him no. But who was Iverley to say what she could or couldn't do? Particularly now, when they were no longer even friends.

He looked at her as though he were surprised she should have the temerity to demand an explanation after his grave pronouncement. She raised her brows and regarded him impatiently.

"He's dull," he sputtered after a moment. "He has no sense of humor. He's . . . he's not right." He enumerated the reasons on his fingers, then stopped and scowled at her. "Very well. Do what you want. It is certainly no business of mine."

She stood to her feet. "No. It isn't." Her attempt at a grand exit was ruined when he followed her. "I asked you to leave me alone," she snapped, whirling back to face him.

"What did you tell him?" His voice was low.

"Ask him. Ask anyone. You should know better than anyone that these kinds of things rarely stay private for long." She moved toward the house, cutting across a large circle of paving stones that were raised in the form of a stage. She had hardly gone three strides before his hand clamped hard on her elbow. She ignored the flush of desire that raced across her skin at his touch.

"What did you tell him?" he repeated. His hazel eyes glinted with a dangerous fire.

There was a long pause filled only with the hiss of water. "No," she said at last. "I said no."

She was watching his expression closely, but it showed her nothing. What was she hoping for? Joy? Relief?

"Why?"

She shook off his hand at her elbow. The numbness inside her was simmering into anger. How could she tell him that she had said no because she was still more than half in love with him? And that she now knew, ever since that day at Biddling Wells, that the Vaughn Iverley she had thought herself destined for had been entirely a product of her overheated imagination. "You wouldn't understand," she replied, giving an impatient shrug.

"Tell me why." It was an imperious command now. He had taken her by both shoulders and was standing toe to toe with her, towering over her. His dark brows nearly met in the middle in an expression calculated to intimidate her.

Her heart felt like it would fight its way out of her body, but outwardly she preserved a calm mien. She enunciated each word clearly to be certain he understood. "Lord Iverley, I'm going back to the house." She jerked out of his hold and stalked away across the dais.

She should have recalled what the black paving stones meant, but she was too furious. When she saw it at the last second, she had already put her foot down on it.

A jet of water shot up and over her head. Then, a jet on the other side of the round flat dais in which they had stopped spurted an arch in the other direction. A third on her left side did the same. She saw now that there were little spouts spaced every few inches all the way around the platform. They sprang up one after another in a glissando of water. She turned frantically, looking for a way to get out before they were trapped inside the arches of water on all sides. "Go! Go!" she cried, pulling at Iverley's sleeve.

It was too late. In a moment, they were fenced in on all sides by shining streams of water.

"Hm, a kind of liquid gazebo," Iverley said mildly, looking up to where the jets crossed and recrossed over their heads.

"More like a cage. There must be a way to turn it off. How could there be a way to turn the stupid thing on from the inside without a way to turn it off?"

Tomlinson had probably built the water gazebo as a secluded place of romance. The man was obviously out of his mind. It was cold, dark, and imperfectly designed. She jumped back from a clogged nozzle that was spraying water toward the inside of the water dome, only to find that at the middle of the dais, a steady stream of water poured down from where the streams of water clashed overhead. The cool night air suddenly felt freezing.

"Help me!" Georgiana pushed her wet hair out of her eyes and continued stamping on any black paving stone she could find. "Why won't this dreadful thing turn off?"

She was strangely frightened. They were so cut off from the rest of the world. It was just the two of them, alone.

The torches and lamps in the garden seemed blurry and weak through the veil of water. Their fuzzy halos of light looked as far away as stars, and in contrast made Iverley seem very near and very dark. She turned away from him.

It was dangerous in here. Iverley was angry and in no mood to play the gentleman. He stood exactly where he had been when the water turned on, arms crossed, scowling.

"This is ridiculous," she sputtered. "We shall have to run through the water to get out and then we will be soaked. A fine thing that would look, going back into the ballroom. Tomlinson and his wretched inventions! I shall have a thing or two to say to him when we get back. My gown's quite ruined."

She held her skirts out to keep the dripping silk from clinging to her legs. It was becoming quite indecent, really. She was glad of the dim light, but at the same time was vividly aware of Iverley's gaze. Tension hummed in the air between them.

"Well, I suppose I will go first. There is no sign of this wretched thing stopping on its own." She was aware that she was babbling, but Iverley merely continued to stand there and look at her with an inscrutable expression. She steeled herself to jump through the cold wall of water.

Just as she was about to leap, Iverley stepped over and took her arm. Somehow, his warm grasp was paradoxically calming and upsetting at the same time.

"Why did you say no to him?" he asked again, just as though they were standing in a drawing room rather than being spattered with icy water in a madman's garden.

"You wouldn't understand," she said through chattering teeth.

He continued to look down at her, his eyes steady and unreadable.

"You care nothing for love," she went on, well aware that she was no longer acting like the jovial, level-headed Georgie he knew. But she didn't care. It didn't matter anymore. "For you love isn't necessary when it comes to marriage. For you it is nothing but a business arrangement or something unpleasant that must be done, like having a tooth drawn."

"And for you?" His face was so close to hers that their noses nearly touched.

She tried to pull away from him. "Please get me out of here. I'm feeling extremely uncomfortable with all this cold water, and this . . . this closeness."

Somehow her attempt to move away had only brought her closer to him. They were standing now in what could only be called an embrace. Water diamonds sparkled on his coat and in his hair. One of his mahogany curls was drooping over his eye with a heavy drop of water beading at the end.

"You don't love him," he said softly.

"What?" she raised her eyes from his mouth to his eyes, and found she had forgotten entirely what they were talking about.

"You don't love him," he repeated, his voice low and soothing. "And you're not going to marry him."

The drop of water fell from his hair onto her lower lip. He reached out to wipe it away, his thumb crossing her mouth, slightly open from shock, and then lingering there. "No." The word came out almost a whisper.

"And you didn't kiss him." Those snake charmer eyes had bewitched her. She couldn't move, even when his fingers moved to push her damp hair from her temple.

"No, of course not," she said with a feeble attempt to rally herself out of this dreamlike state. His hand against her back brought her up against his chest.

"You're going to kiss me." It wasn't a command or a request, it was only a statement.

For a moment she only stared at him, stupidly unable to comprehend the outrageousness of his presumption. And then his lips touched hers.

"Wait . . ." Her denial was pathetically weak, even to her own ears. It sounded almost pleading, as though she wished for him to kiss her. And she found her lips moving against his, as though she wanted it more than anything. With one arm wound around his neck and the other dragging at his lapel, her body demanded more. The rational part of her mind made a last whimpering protest then retreated in defeat.

His mouth was warm against hers, tasting of cold water, brandy, and mystery. Just when she thought she could stand it no longer, he began again, this time touching his tongue to her lips, and then, in a way that was both alarming and erotic, to her own tongue.

Did all men kiss like that? In paintings and sculpture, it only looked like people pressed their lips together. She hadn't really realized there could be more to it. She pressed against him, fiercely returning his passion.

Then, all at once, the water fell away, and there was silence.

Georgiana drew a quick, painful breath and stepped back. Reality was cold and wet. She wrapped her arms around herself, feeling utterly exposed. A suddenly icy breeze slashed against the soaked clothes that she realized were clinging to her in the most shocking manner.

Iverley, too, looked around him with an expression of surprise. Then he smiled in a slightly bemused way, as though he himself were just waking from a spell. "Well," he said, after a long, strange silence, "I suppose we had better go inside."

Sixteen

Iverley prowled the room at the inn, idly picking up and putting down teacups and disorganizing the pretty bunches of hothouse flowers that had been sent to his sister after the Tomlinsons' ball.

He was going mad cooped up in here. The dawn had dragged in a mass of black clouds that had settled down to release a steady pour of rain all morning. There was no question of hunting or driving and no hope of receiving visitors.

He pulled a drooping lily from a bouquet and used it to scrub a peekhole in the foggy windows. For some reason watching the rain spill from the eaves of the stables reminded him of fountains, which reminded him of water gardens, which made him uncomfortable.

What cog had gone loose in his head last night? Why hadn't he kissed her long before, back when they were thick as inkle weavers? Why had it happened last night, when she'd given every indication that she didn't want it?

He crushed the flower head against the windowpane. His timing was abominable. She'd moved on, found new friends and new admirers. Why couldn't he let her go, as she had let him go? He twirled the mangled flower between his fingers and stalked across the room.

He'd told himself that he'd merely missed her company. But it was worse than that. It felt alarmingly like that unnamable affliction that ended one in the parson's mousetrap.

He tromped back to the window and assessed the pocked mud pit that had been the stable yard. A young stablehand dashed out from the inn, his coat over his head and his unlaced boot making great splashes in the puddles. Far too sloppy for anyone to drive over from Coningsby Hall today.

Caro looked up from her sewing and frowned. "Do stop roaming about. You'll drive the poor people below us mad with all that tromping up and down."

He threw himself on the settee and sighed. "That's the problem with the countryside. When it rains there's nothing to do. All the pleasures of country life are in being outdoors. At least in London, one can go to the club and be assured of meeting someone to talk to."

"And heaven forbid you talk to me," she replied mildly.

"It isn't that." He got to his feet again and went to stoke the fire, which was already blazing. "I'm just tired of being cooped up."

"And you're blue-deviled," she supplied. At his protest, she merely took up her sewing again and smiled. "Well, I don't blame you. It is dreary being trapped at this inn. One can never be really comfortable. You should have taken a house for the autumn."

He put the poker back into the stand. "Perhaps so, but I never really intended to stay as long as I have." He hadn't. It was to have been only until the scandal died down in Town. Had he really intended to marry Muriel St. James? The idea seemed ludicrous now.

Caro reached over and took up her teacup. "And I know you stayed on *solely* for my sake." He looked at her to see if she was quizzing him, but her expression was blandly innocent.

He'd kissed Georgie Palmer. What an incredibly imbecilic thing to have done. He had come snapping at her heels like a jealous schoolboy and then, in a moment when she had no way of escaping . . . But he couldn't bring himself to feel terribly guilty. Not when she had responded so passionately. Not when she had fit herself so perfectly into his arms.

She had had every right to slap him for his impertinence. He'd hardly wooed her correctly. He hadn't spoken to her for weeks, except to accuse her of flirting with Hennings. How could he explain to her that he'd needed the time to sort out his feelings? Now he knew what they were, but he still didn't know what to do.

He should have proposed right then in the garden. It would have been the proper moment. After all, one couldn't very well disappear into the dark unchaperoned for three-quarters of an hour, return soaking wet and decidedly disheveled, and expect the world to believe that nothing had happened. Especially when something very definitely had.

But Georgie would have had none of that. Even he knew that one couldn't avoid a woman for weeks, then chase her down in a garden, kiss her, and expect her to accept your proposal of marriage. He wasn't even certain he'd intended to propose. Certainly before that kiss he had not. Afterward? Afterward he was so stunned he didn't know what he thought.

Georgie had regained her senses before he had. Before the water had even drained away down the channels cut in the dais, she was once more the practical, unflappable creature who had come to his aid in the woods so long ago. She'd merely shrugged and smiled and suggested they go and try to find Emily.

Fortunately Georgie's sister was still in the garden and was so splashed herself that when they walked back into the ball, no one seemed to question Georgie's story that they had been caught by surprise by one of the many fountains.

"Really, Vaughn, you are daydreaming!" Caro set down her teacup and stared at him. "Perhaps it is true then what they are saying."

He dragged his gaze from the raindrops rolling down the window. "What are they saying?"

"That you have stayed here this autumn because you are in love with Miss Palmer."

The name gave him a jolt. "In love with Georgie?" he repeated stupidly.

Caro continued sewing with every appearance of placidity. "I said it was nonsense. After all, you've hardly seen her in weeks."

"Only twice in three weeks." How could he explain to Georgiana that he had changed his mind? That he understood what she had meant about Fate and love. How could he tell her that he loved her? He realized at that moment that he did. He loved her.

His sister was oblivious to his revelation. "And everyone knows that she is my particular friend. If you pay her any special attention it is surely only because of that." A faint smile might have crossed her face, but it was gone so quickly he could not be certain. "As she is the sister of your friends, there is every reason that you should show her extra courtesy." She examined her stitches with a critical eye. "And with so many acquaintances in common," she added, "it is not surprising that you would often find yourselves at the same events." As though this settled the question entirely, she put down her work and got up to search her sewing basket for more thread.

"She's changed in recent weeks," he mused. "I used to think her quite the tomboy. More like William and Richard than a girl, really. But then, perhaps because she met you, she seemed to go all ladylike." She had become quieter, more subdued. At the dinner party at Coningsby Hall she'd talked about novels and poetry more than hunting. And she'd looked at him with a strange, sad, almost defiant expression, as though she were determined to put him off.

He wouldn't let it happen. Not now, when he'd finally come to his senses. Georgie was the only woman he'd ever met whom he really felt he could talk to. The only woman who really seemed to understand him. He had been slow enough to realize it, but he wasn't going to let her slip away from him now.

"Indeed, she is not at all the kind of woman I would have thought you would marry," said Caroline. "Of course she has become a very dear friend, and I want her to find a husband who will make her happy, but I think you are far too different to suit." She frowned at her embroidery thread. "Are these two blues the same? I was quite certain that I bought both a turquoise and an aquamarine, but now I see that they are exactly the same. How bothersome. Vaughn, look at these in the light and tell me they are not the same."

He cast an impatient eye over the floss in her hand. "They're both blue. What do you mean we are too different? We are very alike. Incredibly so." He remembered with a sense of nostalgia those early days when they'd first met. They had seemed to share everything in common. There wasn't a word that came out of her mouth that he didn't agree with. She seemed to know his thoughts before he even said them. "We like all of the same things and agree on nearly everything."

Caroline looked perplexed. "You seem to me to be very different. She is so very intellectual."

"Georgie?" He blinked in surprise. "Of course she's clever. Can calculate the odds on a horse in a trice. Besides"—he narrowed his eyes at his sister—"are you implying that that is where our differences lie?"

Caro laughed. "Of course not. I know you were quite the top of your class at Oxford. It is only that you don't seem to care about those kind of bookish things. And she does." She moved to the window and examined the threads again. "Exactly the same. And I did so hope for aquamarine." She sighed. "And no hope of going to the shops today."

"So she's bookish and I'm a dullard. Otherwise, we like all the same things."

Really?" said Caro. "I suppose she does enjoy hunting. But nonetheless, I would pick a different husband for her."

He sat upright on the settee. "Like who? Hennings?"

She looped the threads carefully around her hand and sighed. "No, not Hennings," she said thoughtfully. She put the floss back into her workbox and carefully folded up her sewing. For an infuriating moment he thought she'd closed the subject.

"Georgiana needs a man who loves her," she said at last. "Really loves her. Most women would rather be married to someone, anyone, than chance never being married at all. But Georgiana is different. She doesn't care for society or titles or being the mistress of some grand house. She would rather have a gentle, kind sort of man, than one who is rich and dull. Of course she is so very sweet and beautiful that I cannot see that she will be in any danger of being on the shelf."

Someone gentle and kind? For dashing Georgie? Obviously Caro didn't know Georgie as well as he did. He got to his feet. Besides, he was gentle and kind.

"Oh look!" she exclaimed, her attention caught by a commotion in the courtyard. "Mr. William Palmer is here. He said he would come visiting, but I thought for certain that the rain would put him off. He was talking last night about a trip to Skegness. He and his brother have a little sailboat they want to go out in."

Iverley looked out the window and saw that William had not brought Georgie with them. He returned to pacing the room.

Caro bustled about, righting the room and chattering happily. "Wouldn't that be great fun? A sailing expedition? The boat is quite a little thing, he said. Small enough that a man could sail it by himself. I do hope it isn't raining tomorrow. We could go then."

"I don't see why I wouldn't be a good match for her," Iverley burst out. "I mean, someone like me, anyway."

Caroline stilled and she looked at him with a surprised expression. "Georgiana and you? I suppose I never gave it any serious thought." She appeared to consider it for a long moment then shook her head. "She's a very sensitive and romantic woman. All the things you claim to disdain."

He laughed heartily. "I don't know what kind of faradiddle she's been feeding you. Most likely you think she's like that because you're like that. I know Georgie much better than you do, and she certainly isn't into all that romantic rot. She's a great gun. No nonsense about her. If I were creating the perfect woman, it would be one like her."

"High praise indeed." Caro smiled. "I never thought I would hear those words from you."

The memory of Georgiana's mouth against his own surged up again. "If I were to ever marry, it would be to someone like her."

Caro looked innocently confused, but there was the ghost of a smile behind it all. "But not her?"

"Well," he sputtered, "that is . . . I would like it to be . . . I mean . . . Well, I don't know if she—"

Caroline looked at him with an expression of supreme satisfaction. "It's all right, Vaughn," she said soothingly. "I understand entirely."

Seventeen

"It was Weatherby."

"No, it was Granger. Weatherby's crew was disqualified. Don't you recall?"

"No, no," said Richard. "Weatherby was disqualified in '12. He won the cup in '13. I was there, Will, I should know."

The fascinating debate as to who had won the Henley Regatta had lasted all morning. One would have thought that a conclusion could have been reached in the several hours it took to reach Skegness, but her brothers continued to argue the matter even as they walked down the sandy path to the beach.

Georgiana had tried to bow out, claiming that she wished to spend time with her mother, but Mama had encouraged her to go, since she had planned a watercolors expedition with Eugenia Harwell.

"Likely more drawings of birds," she muttered, trailing behind the crowd as they walked down the path. "She'd rather go bird-watching than save me from this." Her mother had given her an arch look this morning, as though she were anxious to throw her and Iverley together. After all, they had spent so much time in each other's company previously that she could not blame the woman for her expectations. No matter how deluded.

Georgiana felt like a fool. She couldn't even look at Iverley without blushing. And he made matters worse by watching her with that intent expression. Why couldn't she act like the sophisticated London ladies he undoubtedly knew? Most likely kissing in gardens went on all the time at fashionable London parties, and no one gave it a second thought.

She herself had probably already given it a hundred second thoughts. And each one made her more miserable. Two weeks ago, she would have given anything to have been kissed by Iverley. It had been the goal of this whole masquerade, after all. Now the bittersweet memory of it merely emphasized what she had lost.

She crossed the broad band of beach to join the others and drew a deep, bracing breath. It was the perfect day for sailing. The wind, steady and strong, scuffed the surface of the water with white streaks. Still, she wished they hadn't decided to come today. She wasn't ready to see Iverley. She wasn't yet sure her face didn't still hold the vacuously enraptured expression from the night he'd kissed her.

Iverley turned around and looked at her, but she quickly dropped her eyes to the large hamper of food she was carrying. He came over and took it from her, then stood there, shifting awkwardly and clearing his throat. She pretended great interest in the horizon.

Was there ever a time when they had seemed easy with each other? Their comfortable days of driving together seemed like a long time ago, indeed.

"There she is!" Richard shouted. "Isn't she a beauty?" He pointed beyond a pile of rocks to where a tiny sailing boat was pulled up on the sand. "We call her *The Missus*. And a crabby little old thing she is too. Too near the wind and she jibes good and hard. Boom swung around and nearly took my head clean off last time."

"Not that you were using it," Emily piped up.

Richard promptly picked up his youngest sister and threatened to throw her into the water. "She's a lovely craft," he continued over his shoulder. "We worked weeks to repaint her. Quite dashing, I think."

"It's much smaller than I thought it would be," Caroline said, in a voice of disappointment as she obediently admired its white and red hull.

"Nonsense," said Richard, "it's much more fun. Nearer the waves. You really get a feel of the water."

"That's the part I'm not so keen on," she muttered.

Richard laughed. "Come on, Georgie, let's you and I have a go to show them how it's done. There isn't room for more than two, so we shall have to take turns."

"Oh no, let someone else go first," she demurred. But William had suddenly become very devoted to helping Caroline unpack the picnic basket, and Emily was searching for shells. Iverley was looking at her with that peculiar expression that made her heart pound painfully hard in her chest.

She pulled her pelisse closer around her throat and trotted after Richard.

She had always loved sailing. She'd spent many happy summers sailing with William and Richard in the modest lakes near their home. It was likely a good deal different on the sea than on a lake, though. Certainly, the boat seemed much smaller than the other crafts that were zigzagging around the point.

However, her brother was undaunted, and with a little bit of scrambling and shoving they were off. "See?" he shouted to the group on the shore. "Easy as pie.

And Georgie wouldn't have gotten nearly so splashed if she hadn't waded out. She should have let me carry her, but she is far too stubborn."

The wind was fresh and cold. Georgiana inhaled deeply and grinned. Now this was something she really liked. Certainly better than shooting or standing for hours at an interminable race meet. Hunting, actually, she'd gotten to be rather fond of, but this was far, far better. They were skimming across the waves. The wind caught her hair, pulled it from its pins and made her dress flap wildly around her ankles. Mama would be horrified that she'd left her bonnet on the beach, but it was so pleasant to feel the fresh air on her face.

"There now, mind those rocks," Richard called out to her. "Treacherous things. They go out much further from the point than you can see, and you come upon them very quickly. Prepare to come about."

She dragged her eyes from the beach and followed her brother's instructions. "Are you certain it isn't too late in the year for sailing?" she asked as the boat swung around and they both ducked the boom. "We seem to be the smallest boat out here by far." The wind seemed to be blowing more strongly and the skin of clouds that had matted the sun all day had thickened. "The wind has come up a bit."

"Nonsense. It's as warm as a bath today. Perfect day for sailing. The more wind the better. Must take advantage of a day like this. In another two weeks it will be too cold to go out."

The Missus climbed a wave and then nosed down into the trough. Georgiana stifled the urge to shout in exhilaration as a wash of spray spattered her forest green pelisse and beaded on the sable trim. "It is a fine day," she echoed, smiling in spite of herself. The lines hummed in the wind and the little red flag at the top of the mast popped like a whip in time to the tuneless song. Perhaps things were not so bad.

She squinted back at the figures on the shore. It was hard to tell which one was Iverley. See, she congratulated herself, she was over him already. Yes, it would all work out all right. Iverley would wonder for a while why she'd suddenly devolved into a demure, poetry-reading miss, but he'd forget. He'd never know how she'd plotted to deceive him and there would be no lasting damage done.

The ache behind her ribs would go away sooner or later.

Richard looked up at the sail and assessed the distance to shore. "All right, prepare to come about again. Careful, it will be quick. Bravo. You're getting quite good at this. We'll make a Corinthian out of you yet, Georgie."

She made a noncommittal noise in her throat.

"Iverley seems to be in a rather foul mood," she said nonchalantly.

Her brother tightened a line and looked up to gauge its effect on the taut belly of the sail. "See that little bit of flapping there at the edge"—he pointed—"we'll want to adjust enough to get rid of that." Georgiana had given up hope of getting his attention when he finally spoke up again. "Iverley. Yes, I suppose he was rather quiet on the way out. But you can't expect a man to speak his mind about everything."

"I suppose not."

She tried to steady her breath and tell herself it didn't matter. The night of the kiss had merely been a rut in the road of their friendship. An anomaly. The expression on his face when he looked at her was merely bewilderment at finding her so changed from the Georgie he thought he knew.

"Strange though," Richard volunteered unexpectedly. "He said the same thing about you."

"What?"

"That you seemed to be in a foul mood." He let the sheet run out between his fingers a few inches. "If that's what love is, being in a foul mood all the time, I believe I'll steer clear of Cupid's arrows."

"I'm not in love." She'd meant to say it firmly. Laughingly even. But instead it came out sounding a little desperate.

"Oh, certainly not." Her brother drew out the words, with sarcasm. "I'll assure the gossips that they've all been mistaken in the matter."

It didn't matter what everyone thought. If she and Iverley were unhappy, it was not because they were in love. It was because they had discovered that they never could be.

"Shall we go in?" Richard asked, looking slightly disappointed that she had not risen to his bait. "I'll bet William's mad to take Mrs. Markham out. I think he's a bit sweet on her. She swears she won't go, but I daresay he can convince her. Then she can go all squeally, and he can pretend to rescue her. Such rot. After all, what is the point in coming all the way here, if you are not to go out?"

There was no putting it off forever. They would have to go back sometime. Besides, she reminded herself, she had promised herself that she would act naturally now. How hard could that be? It should be much less effort than pretending she gave a rap over things like who won the Henley Regatta in '13.

"Yes," she said, "let's go in, but do remember to take Emily out, too. She was dreadfully disappointed that you didn't bring enough men."

"Enough men? Oh, don't be ridiculous. This isn't a

dinner party or some such thing. She can always throw herself at Iverley's head." He squinted at her. "Since you're so certain you're not in love with him."

"Oh certainly," she assured him quickly. "We're merely friends." Friends who had kissed each other.

They tacked closer and closer to shore, and Georgiana felt her anxiety grow. How ridiculous that she should be nervous! She had only to act like herself. And not wonder about what he thought of her. And not recall that kiss.

She braced herself as the boat hissed up onto the sand. It tipped over to the side on its stubby keel, and she clambered out.

"Next passenger!" she sang out. "I believe you've been singled out for the honor, Caroline."

"I think you and I should go, Lord Iverley," Emily interjected. "If you leave me here, William and Richard will doubtless take the first opportunity to throw me into the sea. You would be very sorry if I were drowned, and so should I, since this muslin cost near nine shillings a yard."

Iverley made a manful attempt not to smile. "I'm afraid I don't know how to sail," he admitted. "Unless you do, the muslin might be a great deal more endangered under my care than your brother's."

Emily wrinkled up her nose. "No, I don't know how to either. Well that's no fun. I shall be obliged to go out with William. And he will go on about ropes and lines and all kinds of nautical nonsense."

"Sheets," William corrected automatically.

Georgiana laughed at the quarrel that arose, since it was the same one they always indulged in and ended, as usual, with William and Richard grabbing her sister and threatening to throw her into the water. Georgiana retrieved Emily's bonnet from the waves and brushed the sand from it. She looked up suddenly when a shadow fell across her path.

"Miss Palmer," Iverley said in a strangely formal voice, "now that you have returned, perhaps you would consent to walk with me along the shore. We could look for seashells. Or something," he added with a boyish shrug that destroyed his proper mien entirely. "I did not grow up near the seashore, so I'm not entirely certain what it is that we should be looking for."

"I believe shells are considered most appropriate," she replied, infusing her voice with so much naturalness that it sounded entirely false. "Or shipwrecked sailors," she added with a laugh that quavered nervously.

"Grand idea," said William. "I know you had particularly expressed an interest in shells, Mrs. Markham. Shall we walk along the beach?"

They started out together, but Caro and Will seemed much quicker at finding what they wanted, and they were quite soon a long way ahead. For once, Georgiana wished her family was not quite so casual about chaperoning.

The waves rolled in, long and flat. They started out as a ridge a long way out then seemed to speed up and grow as they raced toward the shore. There was a moment, just as they crested, that the sunlight was behind them and Georgiana could see the seaweed, bits of wood, sometimes even fish that had been sucked up into the waves. Then the water doubled over and threw itself onto the hard-packed sand of the shore, scattering everything inside it. She knew the feeling of being flotsam caught in a wave. But she had escaped it, she reminded herself. She was in control now.

The lack of conversation between her and Iverley was becoming excruciating.

"Come look at this, Georgie," he said at last, pointing at something near the water.

She walked over and peered into the bubbles of froth fizzing at the waterline. "A piece of sea glass," she exclaimed. She picked up the rounded lump of blue. It had been tumbled about against the sand so long that it was smooth and clouded with a silvery patina. "Very pretty." She handed it to him.

He examined it for a moment, turning it over and over in his hand. "An unusual blue. It reminds me of your eyes." He slipped it into his waistcoat pocket.

Her throat felt for a moment as though it had closed entirely. "Iverley," she chided with a strangled laugh, "you will ruin your reputation for being unromantic."

He started to say something, then abruptly closed his mouth. They continued up the beach, pretending great interest in the mats of seaweed and phlegmy curds of foam the sea had hawked up on the beach.

"I was thinking, Georgiana," he said at last, his voice dangerously serious, "I thought, perhaps—"

"Oh look at this rock. Isn't that unusual?" She leaned down and picked it up. It was very much like the rest of the rocks on the beach. "It's peculiar how there are great stretches of sand then all of a sudden you run across these banks of stones. All clumped together." She was suddenly very afraid of what he was going to say. There was an expression on his face that had to be stopped before he did something he would hate her for.

"I suppose thousands of years from now, they'll all be sand too," she continued, when he opened his mouth to reply. "It's lovely how they become all smooth. Just like cobblestones." She rubbed her fingers across the rings of strata circling the rock. "It wears them away in such lovely designs."

"Yes," said Iverley, with a faint, deflated sigh.

The water clattered across the rocks, tumbling and rearranging them with every new wave.

"I do enjoy the seashore," she said, feeling like a fool. "It's a pity the weather is not better today. But I suppose we must take our pleasure while we may. After all, it is not often that one can go sailing so late in the year. But it would be so very disappointing if, after such a drive, our sailing should be put off for rain."

He was smiling and nodding, trying to help her. "Yes, it would be too bad if it rained."

Why couldn't she stop thinking about that kiss?

"I suppose we could just have lunch at an inn and then drive back, but it would be disappointing indeed," she babbled on. "But I daresay it will hold off for a little while longer."

"Georgiana, there's something I—"

"At least we brought the closed carriage. If it does rain."

He looked at her for a long moment, assessing her. "Yes," he said at last, "there is that.

The shells that caught his interest after that seemed to draw him quite a long way away from her.

"Did you see us?" Richard demanded as the little boat plowed up onto the beach. "We went right under the bow of that ketch! Another moment and they would have run us over! Emily was screaming her head off. But I daresay we were never in too much danger." He leapt out and splashed up the sand, pulling the boat into the shallows. "Who's next? Will? Mrs. Markham? Iverley? You haven't gone yet."

"You will not get me on that little thing," Caroline said firmly. "I have no wish to be doused with cold water, nearly run over by boats, or tossed about by the wind. I should likely disgrace myself by being ill."

Richard looked nonplussed. "Oh. All right then. Though it's perfectly safe you know. At least, mostly. How about you, Iverley? Fancy a go?"

"I'm afraid sailing isn't one of my accomplishments," he demurred.

"Nonsense. A fine sportsman like you?" Georgiana laughed, going over to the boat. "Why even I know how to sail, and I am certainly not a great Corinthian like yourself."

"Well, Georgie, you have certainly gone to extreme lengths to show me that you can do everything I can. I should certainly make an effort to learn to sail. I had no idea my education was so shockingly lacking."

"If you wish me to teach you, I should be happy to," she replied. She immediately wished she hadn't said it. They hadn't been alone since he'd kissed her.

But it was too late to retract her invitation, and she found herself obliged to climb clumsily into the little cockpit with him. Had the boat always been so small? With Iverley's height and breadth, it seemed suddenly more intimate than it had been when she sailed with her brother.

"Now, I'm afraid you'll have to sit beside me," she said in what she hoped was a businesslike tone. "We must use our weight away from the wind."

"So, one false move, and we shall be capsized?" he quizzed her.

"No, it isn't quite like that. At least, I don't think so." It was a rather inconvenient time to recall that she had never captained the boat before, having only followed her brothers' directions. She hoped William's nautical lectures had seeped into her head somehow. "Here, now we're off. Isn't this grand?"

She kept up a steady stream of inane conversation, talking about the principles of sailing, the proper way to come about, the names of the different parts of the boat.

"Is it always this choppy?" Iverley asked, his knuckles white on the gunwales.

She looked at him and was surprised to see that he was quite pale. She had been enjoying the exhilarating feeling of flying as they plunged down and were buoyed up again like a cork. She slackened the sail so that they slowed somewhat. "Are you all right? Shall we go back? Perhaps you are feeling seasick?" She noticed that the sky had darkened and a light rain now mingled with the spray.

"No, no," he said quickly. "Let's not go back. There's something I want to speak to you about."

She felt her stomach do a little roll that had nothing to do with the motion of the waves. "Iverley, if this has something to do with what happened the other night, please be assured that I haven't given it another thought." That was a complete falsehood, but she forged onward anyway. "We were both likely under a great deal of stress."

"I have thought constantly about it," he said, in a voice so low she could barely hear it above the sound of the wind. "And while it was, perhaps, not the gentlemanly thing to have done, I cannot say that I am sorry that it happened. When I thought that you had accepted Hennings's offer of marriage, I realized that he was all wrong for you."

"Oh don't let's talk about him," she said impatiently. Hennings had looked a little disappointed when she'd refused his proposal, but hardly heartbroken. He seemed to have proposed more out of politeness than from any emotion more passionate. He'd agreed quite readily to bring over some sheet music she'd wanted to borrow, and they had conversed on the same easy terms they always had.

If only the road back to friendship had been so easy with Iverley. She glanced over at him. Poor man, he really was looking quite white.

"He is too dull, too literate, too full of poetry," he continued, as though he hadn't heard her. "You don't want someone flowery like that. Oh dear God, we're going to capsize." He clutched the side of the boat as though he really was worried. "Ah, I suppose we're all right now. How just like Richard to decide to take out his wretched little boat in a gale." He drew several deep breaths and appeared to collect his thoughts. "You are like me, Georgie," he said at last. "You need adventure, and you have no time for romantic nonsense."

"I don't?" she asked with a lopsided smile. They were in the lee of the rocks now and the wind went quiet. She realized then that it had been roaring and that Iverley had been shouting his sentiments at the top of his voice.

"I know you," he said quietly, his voice suddenly intimate in the silence. "I know you better than anyone. You're neck or nothing. You're a born sportswoman. You need someone who will talk to you about boxing, not shower you with fluffy poetry."

She'd hoped she would never have to tell him. But she couldn't let him go on thinking like that. She steeled herself and drew a deep breath. "Iverley, there is something I must confess to you."

Eighteen

Georgiana collected her thoughts, preparing to plunge in. She must admit the whole deception. If she didn't, Iverley would remain deluded, and in another moment he would be saying things he would regret. In the strange silence in the lee of the rocks, the sounds of the waves were hollow against the hull of the boat.

Iverley inhaled deeply and turned his eyes from the rolling of the waves. "I must confess something as well," he said in a rush.

"Vaughn, I must speak first—"

"No—" He tried to reach for her hands, but was forced to grab for the gunwales again. Was he struggling with his thoughts or nausea? Poor man, he looked dreadful. She must get him back to shore, confession or no confession.

"It's starting to rain and the wind is picking up. I'm turning back," she said. She looked up at the thick clots of clouds that were rapidly darkening the sky. "I shouldn't have taken you out for the first time when it was so rough."

"Georgie, you have changed me," he said suddenly, as though the words had been stuck in his throat. "I thought I wanted someone sophisticated and worldly. Someone like Muriel. When she broke off the engagement, I wanted nothing to do with anyone." His eyes were steady and clear in his pale face. "Now I realize that Muriel was all wrong. I need someone more like me. Someone who shares my interests. Someone like you."

"Oh, Vaughn, you don't understand. I—"

He put his hand over hers, where it rested on the tiller. He'd gone from pale to very nearly green. The man probably didn't know he was talking nonsense.

"Don't stop me, Georgie. I must say it," he continued. "If I were creating the perfect woman for myself, it would be you. We are so alike. We were made for each other. In every way. Please say that you'll marry me, Georgie."

No, no, it couldn't have come to that. The words made her feel almost sick with longing. How would she ever have the strength to deny him?

She pulled a line more taut, squeezed her eyes closed for a moment, opened them, and then said it. "I can't."

His hazel eyes opened wider. "You can't?"

It was done. In the very moment she had gotten everything she had wished for, she'd thrown it away. But there was no other choice.

He was looking at her as though she'd landed him a facer. "You can't?" he repeated.

"It isn't as though I don't want to," she said miserably.

He was staring at her, perplexed. "Then why can't you?" His expression changed to one of alarm. "There isn't—there isn't someone else, is there?"

"No, of course not," she said, hating the stricken expression on his face. For a moment though she wished it were as simple as her loving someone else. At least that wouldn't reek of trickery. Her explanation, when she tried to wrap words around it, sounded selfish, conniving, cruel. He was waiting for her explanation.

"I'm a fraud," she blurted at last. "I pretended to be something I wasn't just to impress you."

He jerked back, the expression of hurt deepening to one of shock. For a moment the boat rocked in silence. "I don't know what you're talking about."

She couldn't unsay it now. He deserved to know. A man like Iverley shouldn't be tricked into marriage with a woman with whom he had nothing, absolutely nothing in common.

She looked at the horizon and spoke in a low voice. "The reason we seem so perfectly made for each other is because I contrived it to be that way. I researched the things you liked, what you do, what you think, what you eat, and I made myself into the perfect woman for you."

They had slid past the rocks in the harbor. The sail popped open like a chapeau bras and they were off, plunging across the waves. "Why?" She heard him shout over the wind.

"Because I loved you."

He was silent for so long that she was not sure that he had heard her. The rigging howled a strange, unearthly song in the wind, punctuated by the violent whipcrack of the flag at the top of the mast. At last she turned to him and found his eyes fixed upon her.

"You loved me, so you lied to me?"

It sounded worse when he said it like that. "It was foolish, I know. I just wanted you to like me, and I knew you thought I was a ninny."

The rain was growing harder now. She could see it pecking at the surface of the waves. But she had to explain before they got back to shore and met the others. "I don't like boxing, and I hate shooting and races.

I like hunting a little, but I only took it up to impress you. And driving is all right, but I only did that so that you would think I was dashing."

Her hair had come loose from its pins and was dancing around her head like Medusa's snakes. She pushed it out of her eyes with an irritated gesture. "I like poetry and dancing and needlework. I like writing letters and going to the shops. I like all those drawing room things you hate. We are anything but alike, Vaughn."

"You created this entire persona only to trick me." His voice was flat, emotionless.

"I didn't mean to hurt you."

He did not speak for so long that she began to hope he understood. Then he turned on her. "Ah yes," he said in a voice sharp with sarcasm. "You did it because you loved me. You loved me so much that you cared nothing for my own desires. You cared nothing for my happiness, my own pride. You cared only that you got what you wanted, and you didn't mind how dishonest you had to be to get it."

"Vaughn, that isn't true! I—"

"Of course it's true. How did you have the impertinence to lecture me at Biddling Wells on the nature of love? You know nothing about it." His voice was low and grating. "You accused me of making it a business arrangement, but you have made it something far worse. You didn't even give me a choice."

"That's not true," she repeated, stung. "I didn't trick you into marrying me. That is, I'm not marrying you. I could have married you and gotten everything I wanted, but I'm not going to. I told you the truth."

In the trough of every wave, they plowed up a plume of water that soaked them both. The murky water at the bottom of the boat shifted and sloshed ankle-deep over their shoes.

"You wouldn't have gotten everything you wanted," Iverley snarled, his hands tight on the seat. "You would have gotten a husband who despised you for your trickery."

She pushed the wet hair from her face as a small bubble of righteous indignation swelled up within her. She had been honest. Far too late, of course, but she had stopped things in time. "Well it's a good thing we didn't marry," she shouted above the wind.

"Yes," he echoed. "It's a good thing."

The shore was misty and indistinct in the downpour, but she was suddenly desperate to get back there. One more minute with this man, and she would go mad. Of course she had been wrong. But couldn't he see that she had already been punished for her mistake? She would never have the one thing she wanted. A knot of misery pulled tight in her stomach.

"I'll take you back to shore," she said, hoping the trip back would be speedy. The wind was sawing into her raw skin, and her freezing hands felt gnarled into claws around the tiller. But that was nothing compared to the cold contempt she felt from Iverley.

She guided the boat into the wind, and the sails began to shudder. "Duck now. The boom is going to—"

Iverley, with a fierce scowl, rose up to move to the other side of the boat. In her eagerness to get back to shore, she didn't allow enough time in the eye of the wind. A mean-spirited gust caught the boom and snapped it hard in the opposite direction. Iverley didn't even see it coming.

Georgiana saw it strike him hard on the side of the head. She lunged after him, with a shriek, but it was too late; he'd crumpled and gone over the side.

Nineteen

Iverley was vaguely aware of the fact that he was cold and wet and had a throbbing pain in his temple. He opened his mouth to object but received a mouthful of saltwater for his troubles.

"Oh God, Vaughn, please don't die," a pleading voice said close to his ear. He looked around and realized that both he and Georgiana were in the water. He remembered now what had happened. She must have jumped in after him, the idiot girl.

Georgie clutched him around the chest with one arm, and held the side of the boat with the other. The sail flopped wildly back and forth as the tiller swung, unmanned.

"First you try to kill me, then you tell me not to die," he gasped. It was raining so heavily now that it was hard to breathe even when his head was above water. The pain in his head was at last stoking his wits back to life. He wished it hadn't. "I can't swim."

Her arm tightened around him as he struggled. "I have you. You're all right." She was shouting above the sound of the rain and the flapping sail. They were drifting, shoved by the waves, back toward the large rocks at the point. The black hulks seemed far enough away now, but he could see the waves exploding against their sides and hear the cannon fire of the impact. He wondered what it would sound like if a small sailboat hit them.

He reached up and clutched the side of the boat. It was uncomfortable hanging there by one arm with Georgie still holding him in a death grip, but at least he was thinking more clearly now. The momentary panic had receded. He judged the distance to the rocks and wondered how they would get back into the boat. The little vessel bobbed awkwardly up and down, dragging them half out of the water and then plunging down so that they sputtered and choked as the waves slapped against them.

"I have you," Georgiana said again. He could feel the current as she kicked the water beside him. Even when the boat dragged them up, and he felt himself go heavy against her, she held on to him.

"I told you to duck," she said in a voice he could hardly hear above the wind. "I thought you knew what to do. I'm so sorry, Vaughn, so sorry for everything."

"Later," he snapped. "We have to get away from the rocks."

The sails on the boat above them were flapping wildly, the noise of the canvas like thunder. He looked back toward shore, and realized it was a long way away. There was no way the group on the beach could rescue them. It was unlikely they even knew what had happened.

"Let go of me and get back into the boat," he commanded through the buzzing sound in his head. The sound of the waves on the rocks was close to making conversation impossible. He detached himself from her grasp and walked his hands down the gunwale to give her more room.

She looked at him with an expression of despair that

was almost pleading, then pushed her wet hair out of her eyes and turned back to the boat.

The gunwales were too high. She couldn't pull herself up enough to get over the side. She tried again and again, but he saw her growing exhausted.

The rocks were gleaming with seaweed and water. He saw a seabird settle down and pick at a crevice before a deluge of water frightened it away. The crash of waves was almost deafening.

"We'll have to try something else," he shouted, taking her arm before she tried again. She was a sight so pathetic he nearly laughed in his misery. Her hair was plastered to her head, with the pretty knot in the back now a dripping mass that fell half into the water. The fur trim of her pelisse was matted and clumped, and her lips had gone an alarming shade of blue. "Come on, we'll go at the same time. My weight will pull the gunwale lower, and you'll be able to climb over the side. Then you can help me in."

She gave him a jerky nod, her jaws clenched in determination. There was only time for one attempt. A few minutes more and they would be flung onto the rocks.

They waited together for the boat to slide down the backside of a wave. "Ready? Heave!" It was a clumsy attempt, but he managed to throw his weight down onto the gunwale. The boat tipped toward them, and Georgiana, greatly encumbered by her tangled petticoats, managed to drag herself into the boat.

He was on the point of slipping back into the water when she grabbed him by the back of his coat. For a long moment it seemed as though neither of them had the strength to go any further. He lay there, half in and half out, as slow drops of blood from the cut on his head dripped onto the mahogany seat of the boat. If

Georgiana let go of him, he'd flop back into the water like a large fish. Only he couldn't swim.

A small rock, a pup of the one that loomed over them, poked its head out from under a wave. There was no time. Georgie braced her feet, took his coat in both hands, and hauled. He gave a few kicks and then tumbled in a heap to the bottom of the boat.

She needed no urging to trim the sails and direct them away from the rocks. He heard the keel grate across something submerged as they turned away.

They were silent as the boat picked up speed and carried them docilely toward the shore.

"What the devil were you doing?" he exclaimed at last. "Why did you jump off the boat? That was the most imbecilic thing you could have done. The boat could have drifted away, and I would have drowned you."

Her chin was set in that stubborn look. He'd seen it before when she faced a fence that was too big. But she kept her eyes on the shore and didn't look at him. "What else would you have had me do? You would have died."

It was true. He would have. He didn't know how long she'd held him above the water while he was unconscious. He would have sunk like a stone. He slowly dragged himself up from the bottom of the boat and took his seat beside her. What did she want him to do, thank her?

Now that the danger was over, he remembered their conversation before the accident. She had duped him. She had thought him a sportsman with the brains of a child who could be easily fooled by her little act. It seemed so obvious now. She had been too perfect. Too compliant. Not a word had come out of her mouth that had not been his own.

Georgiana was covered with gooseflesh and her teeth were chattering, but she still did not look at him. He wanted to shout at her, vent his anger at her, but what was there to say? Any protests that came out of his mouth would only make him look more like a fool.

He sat up and dragged off his coat with difficulty. "Here, I know it isn't dry, but at least it will keep the wind off you."

She started to demure, but at his scowl she took the bedraggled thing and wrapped it around her shoulders. Neck-or-nothing Georgie. She'd twined him around her finger like a ribbon, thrown him away, and then had the audacity to save his life. He wondered if she considered the score even now.

They were making good progress toward the shore, and *The Missus,* as temperamental as she'd been before, now seemed ready to please. At least they'd have something to talk about when they arrived. No one would have to know he'd proposed to her, only to find out he'd been deceived. He had no desire for the rest of the world to know of his humiliation.

This had not turned out in the least like he'd planned. He'd woken up this morning convinced that he was the happiest man on Earth. By afternoon he'd planned to come riding triumphantly into town with his new fiancée beside him.

Instead he would come back rejected, furious, and with a lump the size of Gibraltar on the side of his head.

William and Richard, realizing belatedly that something was wrong, splashed out to meet them. "What happened?" William demanded, catching the bow of the boat and drawing it into shore.

"I made a mistake," Georgiana said in a strangled voice. "And Iverley has borne the brunt of it."

Twenty

"What a shocking accident," said Mrs. Palmer. "Your brothers never should have taken that boat out." She raised the field glasses to her eyes and examined a small brown bird in the hedge. "Oh, I already have the wood thrush. Though that is quite a nice one. Perhaps I should consider drawing mine in a hawthorn hedge. What do you think?"

Georgiana leafed back in her mother's folio of drawings and examined the wood thrush. "I think it looks quite well the way you've done it," she said, trying to muster up the necessary enthusiasm. She stared blankly at the page for a moment or two, then shut the book. After yesterday's debacle, it was hard to believe that the world had, indeed, continued to turn.

"Really, I don't know what I should have said to Lord Iverley's mother if her son had been drowned." The bird gave a little hop and then launched itself into the sky. Mrs. Palmer sighed, lowered the glasses, and went to sit by her daughter on the sunny bench in the shrubbery behind Coningsby Hall.

"However," she said, taking the book of drawings and examining the wood thrush with a critical eye, "sometimes the experience of looking death in the face makes a man reconsider what is most important in life. I would not be in the least bit surprised if he did not make a declaration to you, my dear."

It would certainly not be the declaration her mother expected. "Nonsense," Georgiana said cheerfully. "Lord Iverley and I are merely friends." She pulled off her bonnet and looked up at the sky. Today, of course, the weather was perfect. After yesterday's deluge, the heavens were a serene blue and there was barely a breath of wind. Not that the weather had made any difference in yesterday's misery. It had only made things more dramatic. "After all, Mama, you were the one who advised me from the start that we were ill suited."

"Did I?" Mrs. Palmer looked surprised. "Well that was before I knew him. He is the most charming man imaginable. Why just the other day Eugenia Harwell was congratulating me on the prospect of such an amiable son-in-law. 'Eugenia,' I said, 'you have no idea how well suited they are. I never saw a couple with more in common.' To be sure we haven't seen much of him of late, but he is always welcome at our house I hope he knows. I daresay he'll call upon us as soon as his head is mended."

"Mama, I think it would be best if you did not set your hopes in that direction." She put her bonnet back on her head and tied the ribbons. She could never explain that she had had an offer of marriage from the man she loved most in the world, but had replied in the negative.

"You are far too modest," Mrs. Palmer was continuing. "The whole countryside is on ear waiting for the announcement." Her mother frowned at her drawing of a swallow and then cast it aside. "I shall have to redo that one. It *does* look like a currant bun. Really,

Georgiana, you are very fortunate to have caught an agreeable man like Lord Iverley."

"Mama, I have not caught him."

"When it comes to marriage, most women might as well pull a name out of a hat. In my day, a girl might not know her future husband beyond a dance or two." She brought out her pencil and darkened a few lines in the drawing. "I myself had serious reservations about marrying your father."

Georgiana looked at her mother in shock. "Did you? I always thought—"

"Well, my own mama and papa would have been so very disappointed if I had not accepted him. After all, he was considered a very good match."

"But—"

"In the end I found myself as happy as anyone could wish to be."

Georgiana sat back. She'd never really thought about her parents' courtship. They had always seemed perfectly content. Of course they were not at all the type of people who would be so ill bred as to actually quarrel. And certainly not in an open boat in a rainstorm after having nearly been drowned.

"Did you love him?" she asked.

Mrs. Palmer had her field glasses to her eyes again. For a moment Georgiana thought she hadn't heard her question. Then she brought down the glasses and looked at her daughter. "Yes," she said with quiet confidence. "I did. I didn't right away, you know. It didn't strike me like lightning the first time that I saw him."

Georgiana remembered that day on Bond Street when she'd first met Iverley. She'd assumed the lightning had struck him just as it had struck her.

"It grew more slowly, as I got to know him better."

Her mother went back to drawing. "It does not always have to happen at first sight, you know, my dear. It isn't always like it is in poetry."

It was too late now, Georgiana reflected. She had plunged in, passionately sure that she could force Iverley to return her regard, and had been far too impatient to let things develop naturally.

"I never even liked bird-watching," Mrs. Palmer volunteered unexpectedly.

Georgiana stared at her.

"Your papa was always mad for bird-watching. I would go days without seeing him. I started to accompany him, just to have his company, but I must say, in those early days, I thought I would expire from boredom."

"Did you learn to like it?" she asked.

Her mother looked surprised. "Oh dear me no! I always thought it excruciating." She smiled innocently. "But then I hit upon the idea that I would like to draw the birds we saw. It was the most cozy arrangement imaginable. We both did what we liked, and yet we did it together. I'm afraid I've found it hard not to continue in the habit of drawing birds."

Georgiana looked upon her mother with a new respect. It might have been harder to find a way to combine hunting and poetry, but she and Iverley could have found a way. If she had let Fate take its course, they would have found a way. But she'd rushed her fences, and now there was no going back.

"Oh look, there is Mrs. Markham's carriage," said Mrs. Palmer. "Is it time for calls already? Good heavens, it's nearly four! We'd better go in to her directly, or Emily will plague her to death, asking her if she intends to marry William or some such thing. Although," she said, carefully replacing her pencils in their case. "I wouldn't be surprised if he was sweet on her. He was in an absolutely foul mood this morning. Men are generally never in so dreadful a temper as when they are falling in love."

Or when they were falling out of it, Georgiana added silently. It could have been so different. Why did she admit to the scheme to win him? She should have opened her mouth only to say yes to his proposal and then today she would have been engaged to him. Everything would have been different.

"Likely Mrs. Markham has only come to invite you for a drive tomorrow. How fortunate that you've become bosom bows, as you shall likely be sisters soon enough."

Now that the world likely knew of Georgiana's ridiculous plot to entrap Vaughn Iverley, his sister probably thought that the only reason Georgiana had been friendly was to aid in her pursuit of her brother.

Very well. No more thinking about that. She'd done the right thing in refusing his proposal, and now it was time to get on with life. She straightened her shoulders and strode toward the house.

"I don't know what Richard was thinking," Emily was saying as she entered the drawing room. "If he is such a great sailor, you would have thought he would have known it would rain. Though it was very kind of William to drive you back to the inn in the closed carriage. Certainly the coachman could have done it, but Will was quite insistent, wasn't he? I suspect he is quite in love with you. If he asked you, do you think you would marry him?"

"Caro, how nice it is to see you," Georgiana interrupted, going over to Iverley's sister. "We had hoped that you would call."

Caroline rose, looking slightly relieved. "I'm so

happy you're looking well. I was worried you'd catch cold after your dunking yesterday. You poor creature, having to ride home soaking wet. And Iverley was in such a foul mood. You'd think it was your fault he managed to get himself hit in the head. I do apologize for his shocking rudeness."

Georgiana rang for tea and then sat down. Perhaps she was getting ill after all. There was a painful weariness she felt all the way to her bones. It had been her own decision, she reminded herself. She was the one who had decided to tell him everything.

"I hope your brother is faring well?" she asked, carefully nonchalant. "The lump on his head looked quite painful. Did the doctor look at it?" She wished they did not have to talk of him at all, but of course it would not do not to ask. Especially when she had practically inflicted the wound.

"Of course not. You know how men are about doctors. But it looks much better today, and he certainly appears to be as impervious as you are to a good dousing. I don't think it is a good idea for him to go back to London tomorrow, but of course once he gets an idea into his head, there's no stopping him."

"London?" she echoed through the sudden ringing in her ears.

Iverley was leaving. For good. She shouldn't be surprised. In fact, she should likely be relieved. It would mean she wouldn't have to endure his silent loathing. After the way he had looked at her yesterday, she should be glad he had removed himself from her presence.

Caroline twisted her hands and made a face of annoyance. "I know. It's wretched isn't it? It's what I came to tell you. Terribly inconvenient, really, since I can't very well stay at the inn on my own, so there's no choice for me but to go back home."

"Of course you don't have to go home. Stay with us. We would be so happy to have you." She couldn't lose Caroline, too. She'd made it a point not to talk about Iverley with his sister, but she and Caro had had so much else to talk about, it had hardly seemed to matter. It seemed terribly unfair that they would both leave her. Particularly since Caro didn't want to go.

Mrs. Palmer and Emily echoed her invitation, but Caroline was firm. "Oh no, I shall go back to Markham's estate in Cornwall. Besides, it isn't long until Christmas, and then I shall see Vaughn and my parents at the family seat in Gloucester."

"But you detest Markham's old house," Georgiana protested. "Just because your brother is leaving doesn't mean you have to."

"No, I've stayed here longer than I should have." She looked around her with an expression of regret. "Your family has been so good to us both. You have made this autumn so memorable."

Memorable. That was a polite way of putting it.

"Stay until the holidays," she urged. "You can go straight to Gloucester from here." Caro and Iverley gone. The rest of the winter stretched out before her, dreary and lonely. "Please don't go."

"You're very kind to offer," Caro said with a laugh. "I must say, at the moment I am too annoyed with Iverley for ruining my plans to consider anything."

Georgiana directed her attention to the tea tray that was brought in. "Why is he going?" she asked, with a peculiar squeak in her voice.

"Oh I'm sure I don't know," Iverley's sister replied. "He never even mentioned the idea until this morning. I'm surprised, since after the debacle with that St. James woman, he had said he had no desire to ever set foot in London again. And we were having such a good time here. He seemed completely content to stay until Christmas." Her hazel eyes, so like Iverley's, were suddenly upon her with an expression of speculation. "And I must say, everyone thought that you and he—"

"Not in the least," Georgiana said, infusing her tone with an overabundance of cheer. "Isn't it a fine day today? We shouldn't stand on ceremony and stay indoors. Mama and I were just enjoying a walk in the shrubbery, but it would be ever so much more pleasant if we all went down to the river. I promise I will not end up falling in," she said, with a weak attempt at a joke.

"An expedition! How grand. I'll call for our cloaks," Emily exclaimed, springing up and leaving the room.

Caroline turned to Mrs. Palmer. "And how are your sons, ma'am?" Georgiana thought she saw a faint flush on her friend's cheeks.

"Oh, they've driven into Lincoln to see some prizefight," Mrs. Palmer replied with a gesture of dismissal.

"I expect they'll be back soon, since Mendoza is favored three to one," Georgiana added. "I don't expect Wallace will be able to go more than four rounds. Mendoza beat him in two when they fought last May." As if on cue, there came the sound of Richard's voice as her brothers came in from the stables. She laughed. "I expect they'll be in in a moment with a blow-by-blow account of the whole thing."

Caroline looked slightly bemused. "How do you know so much about pugilism?"

"Well—" She pressed her lips together. "It's something I used to follow. But I don't anymore."

The door to the drawing room banged open. William looked rather disheveled, with his driving coat dusty to the heels and his hat askew. "What's this I hear about you leaving, Caro?" he demanded.

Caroline turned pink and murmured something indistinct. Mrs. Palmer, seeing Emily looking gleeful behind her brother, took this opportunity to excuse herself from the room to attend to urgent family business.

William crossed to Iverley's sister and took her hands. "Why did you not tell me before?" he asked softly.

"Oh dear," Georgiana said in a bright voice. "I just recalled that Mama left her sketchbook out in the shrubbery. She will be distraught if anything should happen to it. I'll just run out and get it, shall I?"

Neither of them noticed as she slipped out of the room.

Emily was watching the drawing room door from the top of the stairs, but Georgiana decided not to join in her vigil. She'd known this was coming of course. Caro and Will were so obviously meant for each other. She wandered back out into the gardens. Mama had indeed left her sketchbook on the bench, so she picked it up and idly leafed through the pages.

Caro and William. It was lovely really. Now that she considered it, she realized they were well-matched. A part of her mind that she didn't want to own cried out in envy. They were in love with each other. It had happened naturally and quietly and mutually. There had been no delusions of grand destiny and no elaborate plot-making. And everything would work out happily for them.

The drawing of a rock dove blurred before her eyes. She rubbed her nose hard. She was happy for them. She really was.

Twenty-one

With a feeling of foreboding, Iverley put his horse over the fence that marked the boundary of the Palmer's land. He'd spent the morning nursing his headache, but he wished he'd decided to go to the mill in Lincoln instead. At least that would have kept his mind off things.

He rode toward the stables at the back of the house, as he always had. It was habit from when he used to run tame in Coningsby Hall. It seemed like a long time ago now.

He couldn't avoid this visit. It had to be done, he reminded himself. No one would think it odd that he was going back to London, but he'd be dammed if he was cowardly enough to go without taking leave of the family that had been so kind to him.

He practiced again a series of pat phrases he would use with Georgie. There would be no cause to be alone with her, so there would be no reason to have to go over, once again, her convoluted reasons for lying to him.

He dismounted and threw the reins to the stable boy. He was just trying to decide whether to go around to the front of the house like a proper guest or to barge in as he always had, when Miss Emily Palmer came out to meet him.

"Hello," she said, looking somewhat surprised. "I heard you were going to London."

"I am. I came to take leave of your mother. I believe my sister is already here?"

Emily seemed to consider this for a moment. "Yes," she said slowly. "But she is having a . . . a private conversation at the moment." Her eyes lit up. "Why don't you go into the garden?"

"All right," he said, slightly confused. What kind of conversation was so private that he couldn't even enter the house?

"I'll join you in just one minute. You can meet Mama in the shrubbery." She waved him off cheerfully and disappeared back into the house.

He stood there for a moment, nonplussed, then obediently strode off into the garden.

In a moment he realized that Emily had set him up, the minx. There was Georgie, sitting on a bench looking at a set of drawings. Her expression was serious, nothing like the wild, carefree girl who took her fences at full tilt and could laugh at any bawdy joke you chose to tell. She looked almost fragile sitting there. She looked grave and quiet, somehow as though she never, ever laughed.

He tried to muster anger, but it felt more like loss. He didn't know her. He knew nothing about her. She was a perfect stranger behind a beautiful and familiar face. What would he possibly say to her? He turned to go.

At the crunch of gravel under his boot, she looked up. "Vaughn!" She said his name with a mixture of alarm and displeasure.

"Hello," he said turning back, with an acute feeling

of foolishness. "Your sister said your mother was here."

"No. She is in the house."

He nodded for longer than was necessary, trying to think of what to say. "I fancied as much."

"I'll take you in," Georgiana said, standing. "Your sister is here, you know." Bright spots of pink stained her cheeks, and her eyes were fixed on the folio she held in her hand.

"Yes. She said she was going to call on you." And then, because he could not help but ask, "Why are you not with her?"

She looked up at him, but must have felt the same jolt he did, for she dropped her gaze immediately. "She is speaking with my brother."

"Ah yes," he murmured. "The private conversation." They stood in silence for a moment, and then she abruptly began moving toward the house. It was hard not to stare at her. She seemed so like the old Georgie, and yet she wasn't. He wanted to elbow her in a brotherly way and tell her to stop pulling the long faces. He wanted to take her in his arms and kiss her in a way that was wholly unbrotherly. But everything was all wrong now.

"Mama will be delighted to see you," Georgiana said after a silence. "And then you can accompany your sister home if she wishes."

"Yes."

They walked on for a moment. "We are told that you are going back to London," she said, her eyes straight in front of her.

"Yes." He didn't need to explain anything to her. What did it matter if she knew very well that she was the reason he was leaving? "I have business there," he heard himself say.

He hadn't realized before how far it was from the shrubbery to the house. Now it seemed like miles.

She cleared her throat. "How is your head?"

"Fine."

Soon this misery would be over. He'd be back in London. No one there would know of this disaster. He could go back to his old pastimes and forget everything that had happened this autumn. The prospect seemed strangely flat.

"And you didn't catch cold from being in the water?"

"No." He shot a look at her profile. "And you?"

"I'm fine."

A lock of hair was dressed to fall against her cheek. As she walked, it brushed against her face. He watched for a moment and then turned away.

The strained silence between them made the noise of the rest of the world seem harsh. The wind hissed through the hedges and a crooked line of geese honked in discord overhead. It would be winter soon. It couldn't be much past five o'clock, but the light was already going. Georgiana appeared absorbed in her own thoughts, but there was a set to her mouth that suggested that she was as uncomfortable as he was.

He shouldn't have come. He could have sent his regrets in a letter and been gone. Seeing her again brought back the tide of longing and humiliation from yesterday. He had wanted to marry her, for God's sake! The tight wires of restraint between them were more than he could bear. Did she have any idea how it felt to be so manipulated? To feel like the object of a strange little experiment?

He could feel the frustration boiling up inside him. "I don't even know you," he exclaimed explosively at last. "I know absolutely nothing about you. Everything about you was manufactured. I was ready to marry you, to spend the rest of my life with you, and all of a sudden I find out that you . . . you aren't *you*," he finished with a sputter.

She slowly raised her eyes to his. "I only wanted to please you," she said in a dull voice. "I tried to tell you so many times. But it never came out right. And then it was too late."

"Does your whole family expect me to marry you?" he demanded, suddenly wondering if the whole Palmer clan was sniggering behind their hands at him.

She was silent for a moment. When she spoke, her voice was thick. "They only know that I . . . admired you."

Her words pierced him with a strange feeling of pain. Why couldn't she have been who she said she was? He had thought himself in love with her. But now he had found that he had fallen for a tantalizingly beautiful but shallow reflection of himself.

"Did you think I was so dull that I could not care for someone who was not exactly like me?" he asked. He recalled his disdain for her at their first meeting. She had wanted to talk about poetry. She had looked at him with adoration in her face. And he had brushed by her with no feeling other than scorn. One kind word on his part, and both of their lives could have been changed forever. But he hadn't bothered.

"No," she said in a small voice. "Of course not."

"You made a study of me. Like I was a dog who could be trained to do what you wanted." He turned on her. "Everything about you was a lie."

She faced him, her blue eyes bright with sudden emotion. "Not everything."

The memory of the kiss they had shared in the water garden rose up like a bubble, but he burst it. It was hopeless. He would never be able to distinguish what had been real and what had been false. He could never bring himself to trust her again.

She stood with her hand on the door. The lights in the windows made the house look inviting and warm in the early winter twilight. The idea of riding back in the cold to the uninviting Gravescross Arms was unappealing.

"Would you like to come in? It will look most peculiar if you don't," she said in a voice that betrayed nothing of her thoughts.

He followed her with reluctance, and they made their way back to the little parlor where she'd always received him. Its familiarity gave him an unexpectedly sweet feeling of nostalgia.

The whole family was there, chattering like monkeys. "Did you hear?" Emily exclaimed, grabbing his coat sleeve and bouncing up and down. "Your sister is to marry my brother! Is that not romantic?"

"Caro?" He looked at his sister in surprise. She nodded at him, her face pink with shy pleasure. William Palmer stood at her side looking inordinately pleased.

He had seen the admiration growing between them, but he had not expected this. For all Caro's advice on the kind of woman he should marry, she was the one to get caught in the parson's mousetrap. How was it that the whole world seemed to know of his ludicrous passion for Georgie, and they had kept their own feelings a secret?

"My congratulations to you," he said, shaking William by the hand. "I see already that you have made her very happy."

Georgie went and kissed her brother and Caro, murmuring her congratulations. In another moment, the whole room was in an uproar again over when the

couple should marry, if they should honeymoon in
Naples or in Bonn, and how soon they could set up
housekeeping in Congingsby Hall.

It was strange, seeing the loving pair from the outside. They seemed so natural together. It was ridiculous he had never considered it seriously before. Caro
could hardly go a moment without reaching out to William to touch him, as if to assure herself that he really
was there. They were confident in their happiness and
seemed to include everyone in the room in it.

In a strange flash, he knew exactly what it would
have looked like if he had proposed to Georgie and
she had accepted. If she had never mentioned her little
plot. There would have been two couples and even
more happy exultation. A brother and sister marrying
a brother and sister. How picture-perfect. But then all
the warm joy in the room would have been built on
falseness. He went to pour out drinks for everyone.

"How's the head, my dear?" Mrs. Palmer slipped
her arm through his. "Are you in terrible pain?"

"Not in the least, ma'am."

"You're lucky you were not drowned. Or worse."

He couldn't actually imagine what worse could have
followed drowning, but he nodded anyway.

"Richard and William were mad to take that boat
out so late in the season. I'm glad you're so hardy."
Mrs. Palmer's look of concern became confiding.
"What do you think about becoming one of our family?"

He started and stared at the woman. "Oh! You mean
Caro and William. Yes, I'm delighted. They seem very
happy." Even after he realized what Georgie's mother
meant, the tingles that danced along his nerves refused
to stop.

Mrs. Palmer patted his arm in a motherly fashion.

"We are delighted to welcome you *both* into our family," she said, with emphasis.

He didn't blame her for her expectations. Hadn't he run tame in her house for the last few months? The attention he'd paid her daughter could hardly go unnoticed. And the sudden rift would be fodder for the gossips. He felt a surge of anger and shame. Georgiana had brought this on them both. Very well. He'd go back to London and leave her to face the embarrassment of his sudden and unexplained indifference.

At last everyone had finished congratulating everyone else. The fire was burning low, and he could see Emily yawning behind her hand. "Come on, Caro, I'll drive you home. Your coachman can ride my animal back to the inn." He rang for the horses while everyone bade their last good-byes. They spilled out onto the front steps while the carriage was brought round, and somehow in all the embraces and kisses, Georgiana came to be in front of him.

She stood there, nervously toying with the fringe of her shawl. "I'm delighted for Caro and Will," she said, unnecessarily.

"I am, too. They make a fine couple."

She stood for a moment shifting from one foot to the other. Her expression was hard to read. Somehow in the joyous crowd, it was only the two of them. And they had nothing left to say to each other.

"Good night, Iverley," she said at last, her voice worn, as though she had grown too tired to care anymore. "I would say that I'm sorry, but I know it would do no good." Her hand twitched as though she were going to offer it for him to shake, but instead she clutched her wrap, twisting the cloth in a gesture of awkward discomfort.

A part of his mind that apparently had no pride

wanted to take her in his arms and kiss the look of misery from her face. But how did he know even that expression was real? "Good night," he said gruffly.

They stood for a moment, looking at each other in silence. "Good night," she said again. Then she turned into the darkness and went into the house.

Twenty-two

There was nothing like getting hit in the face to make one forget one's troubles. Iverley dashed the blood and sweat away from his eyes before plunging back in. Barry was a blacksmith, broad and heavy, but his weight was working against him. Another round or two and he would be bellows to mend. If only he himself could keep from getting killed in the meantime.

He slipped in a doubler followed by a hard dig with the left. Barry grunted. Yes, this was the way to deal with frustration. Vent it on some large stranger. Iverley dodged Barry's right hook and fell back to make the man work for his next attack.

"Come on, lads, keep the muffles up," Jackson shouted from the ringside. "Ye do well enough when you concentrate, Iverley."

A staggering blow to the chin underscored this lack. Iverley shook his head to quiet the ringing in his ears. Barry had an arm like a club. Well, if nothing else, he would have all memory of Georgiana forcibly beaten from his head.

"Softly, Barry. Don't chase him. He'll wear you down." Gentleman Jackson followed them around the outside of the ring. Though it was the middle of the afternoon, a sizable crowd of men had gathered in the boxing salon to watch the practice bout. Barry was a noted bruiser, and those who went up against him generally came out somewhat the worse.

See, Iverley reminded himself, things were now just as they should be. He was back in London living the life of a Corinthian with no romantic folderol to distract him. He noted with satisfaction that Barry's left eye was closing. He'd likely have darkened daylights himself before the match was through, but there was some pleasure in knowing he'd acquitted himself reasonably well.

Besides, turning up in Hyde Park tomorrow with a black eye would ensure that the muslin party would keep their distance. Oh, how Georgie would laugh to see him in this state. He swiped at his cut lip and reminded himself that he had no intention of ever seeing her again.

"Mind, Iverley! Pay attention!"

Jackson's admonishment was too late. He turned to avoid the weight of the blow, but it still landed heavily on his side. He focused his attention. No one would ever again play him for a fool. No woman could be trusted, no matter how highborn or how sweet-faced. He fell on Barry like an animal and rained blow after blow.

"There you go, Iverley!" he heard voices in the crowd shout. "Show 'im!"

He would not think about Georgiana. He would not wonder what she was really like. He would not consider the possibility that the spark between them had been real. He fought on like an engine, pounding the foreign flesh as though he could fight the devils that besieged his mind. He would not recall that kiss.

"Iverley! Iverley, enough, you blood." Jackson had

jumped the ropes and pushed between them. Iverley realized that the round had ended.

He stepped back, panting. The room came back into focus, and the roar of the crowd rushed into his ears. He was shaking with anger and exhaustion. Barry collapsed to his knees with a weak gesture of capitulation.

"I'm done up," he grunted. "Enough for me."

"Neatly done." Pierce Egan, the noted sporting news writer, ducked into the ring and offered both contenders towels. "Jackson, I haven't seen such a fine turn-up in weeks. We'll have these two out to Moulsey Hurst yet."

Jackson took this praise as though it was his due. "You," he said to Barry as he helped him to his feet, "must trim the crummy. You're plump as a pigeon. He ran you off your feet. You'd have had him otherwise. And you"—he took Iverley's towel and applied it hard to the leaking cut on his lip—"you kept losing the head. All in the clouds, thinking of something else. You got it together in the end, but it was all brawn and no science. This is an art form, Iverley. You've got to fight cunningly."

Iverley mustered the strength to nod. He was lucky Barry was blown at the end. Losing concentration like that would have made him an easy target to a more experienced pugilist.

"God, but you're handy with the fives," said a familiar voice as he left the ring. "As good a turn-up as I've ever seen from you."

"Palmer," he said in surprise. "Why are you in town?"

Richard looked somewhat hurt. "You hardly own the place. I thought you'd be pleased to see me."

Iverley turned the towel and pressed it again to his

lip. "I am indeed. Merely an unexpected pleasure, I assure you."

"Got deadly dull at Coningsby Hall after you left. No one talking of anything except bridal clothes. And William smelling of April and May. He looked like a sheep all the time, and the tripe that came out of his mouth . . ." He rolled his eyes. "I had to get out."

Iverley made his way into the changing room, where the next pair of opponents was stripping for their lesson. "I had a letter from my sister yesterday. Filled with the same nonsense. She labors under the delusion that I have an opinion on how many tablecloths would suit and whether she should let a house in town or refurbish the one on Culross Street."

"Are you here in town for Christmas then? I can only stay a week. Must go back to my mother. She's pleased as punch that William is to be shackled next spring. I daresay they'll be leaning on me next."

"How is your family?" Iverley asked, with elaborate unconcern, though he knew they were well. Caro had mentioned as much in her last letter. Though she'd only said so in the most general of terms and then crossed and recrossed dozens of lines about her beloved William.

Iverley ducked his head in a barrel of water to wash off most of the blood and sweat. He'd bathe when he got home, but he couldn't very well traipse down the streets looking as though he'd been turned nearly inside out.

It was gratifying to hear Caro so happy. After all, she deserved a love match this time around. He pictured his sister sitting in Coningsby Hall making wedding plans with the Palmer sisters.

"Oh well enough," Richard was saying when he emerged from the water. "When it wasn't about the wedding, it was about Emily's Season. I never heard anything so dull."

"And Georgiana?" he asked into the towel he was rubbing over his face. Was she unhappy, watching Caro plan a wedding when she could have been planning her own? Or was she immune to any tender feelings? Perhaps she was plotting how she would ensnare her next victim. But he couldn't conjure up any real bitterness. It was mostly a feeling of loss. Things could have been very different.

"Very well," said Richard. "Head in a book, as always. But she does go out to Henning's meets. Got the brush at the last one, actually. She's turned out a bruising rider."

"What does she read?" Why had he asked such a thing? It could hardly be of any moment.

Richard examined the neck cloth he was holding and then handed it to Iverley. "Fine linen. Do you have them imported? I started wearing a belcher, but Mama said she would go off in an apoplectic fit if I continued. Decided they didn't suit me anyway." He seemed to recollect that Iverley had asked him a question. "Oh, Georgie reads poetry, mostly. Damned silly stuff if you ask me. I tried to read some of it, once, when I'd finished the *Weekly Dispatch* and had nothing else to read. Could make neither heads nor tails of it. Don't think I'd mind Byron's stuff so much. At least Georgie says I won't because it's quite scandalous. But Cowper makes my head spin."

Iverley made a noise of assent. He put on his coat, feeling the early twinges of soreness as he felt for the second armhole.

"I say, Iverley, you'll be in full mourning tomorrow." Palmer indicated his blackened eyes. "You should have let him hit one of them twice instead of each of them once." He laughed at this witticism. "But I've never seen you strip better. Always handy with the fives, but today you went beyond."

"Barry's a brute," Iverley admitted, admiringly.

A rather ridiculous part of him wished that Georgiana had been around to see him today. She likely would have laughed heartily to see him so battered, but perhaps, since she did seem to have an appreciation of the art, she would have understood his pride in having bested Barry. Despite his shocking lack of science.

"Did she ever really like boxing?" he demanded.

Palmer looked up. "Who?"

"Your sister," he said, wishing the question hadn't slipped out. "Georgiana."

"Like boxing? I don't know. She went through a phase where she did. Now, she doesn't seem as interested. Though I've seen her reading Egan's column in the *Dispatch*. You were mentioned in it two weeks ago."

"I saw," he said. "He said it was only luck that I beat Kettering."

"He also called you Jackson's protégé."

Iverley shrugged.

"She's an odd girl," Richard continued. "Thoughts all in the clouds. Too romantic by half if you ask me."

They walked out onto the street. It was cold after the heat of the boxing salon. But the weather was fine, so they turned up the street toward Iverley's lodgings on Upper Brooks Street.

"I had half a mind to go to Tatt's while I was here," Richard said. "I heard Mowery was selling his roans. They're a bit small, but I thought they'd do well enough for my curricle. Perfectly matched, which is dashed hard to do with roans. I have my hesitations though. I know Mowery drove them hard last Season, and I can't help but wonder if they're roaring. It would be just like the man to try to pass 'em off if they're broken-winded."

"Too romantic?" Iverley exclaimed, with some disbelief. He saw that Palmer was looking at him with an expression of confusion. "You said your sister, Georgiana, was too romantic."

Palmer looked nonplussed for a moment. "She is. Oh you know how chits are sometimes. Sighing and weeping over books when they think you ain't looking. Taking long walks to view some tumbled-down cottage that is thought picturesque. I have no idea what picturesque means, but I've learned to agree heartily whenever she suggests that something is. Otherwise we'll be there for hours looking at the creepers growing up a wall or the lichen on the stones of some old ruin. I can't tell you how many times I've been dragged to the old baths at Biddling Wells."

Iverley made a noise of assent, his mind racing down avenues he was not entirely certain he was comfortable with. Did she think of him at Biddling Wells? Perhaps he wasn't alone in wishing things had been different.

"Now in all fairness, Georgie is better than most," Richard said generously. "She doesn't go blubbing over silly things like Emily does. In general she's a great gun. Went all over white when we talked about going sailing again next summer with you, but I daresay that was because she was so embarrassed about jibbing the boat like that. She should have known better. But she's so stubborn she doesn't like to admit she doesn't know how to do things."

For once, Iverley was glad that Palmer was a rattle. He made the requisite syllables of interested encouragement and waited for him to go on.

"Once she gets an idea of what she wants, there's no calling her off it. Like hunting. Once she'd decided that she would learn, she stuck with it until she got the hang of it."

Or once she decided she wanted him, Iverley thought. For the first time since she'd admitted her deception, he felt a faint glow of gratification. She knew what she wanted, and she took it. There was no namby-pamby wishing and hoping. And she had wanted him.

For all her talk of love and Fate, perhaps they were not so different after all. They were both strong-willed enough to twist destiny to their bidding.

"And if she does not get what she wants?" he asked, feigning great interest in the bruises forming on his knuckles.

Richard thought for a moment. "Don't know," he said in surprise at last. "I suppose she generally gets it." He considered the matter further as they walked. "She isn't foolish though. Not the kind of girl to cry over the moon when she finds she can't have it."

Iverley reached up and touched the cut on his lip. It had stopped bleeding, but it would be a good while before he could smile without opening it up again. He didn't really foresee smiling much in the near future anyway. "I didn't think she was," he said quietly.

He wondered if he himself would sit passively while Fate passed him by.

"Well, this is your house," Richard interrupted his own chatter at last. "I think I'll trip on down to see if anyone is at White's. Shall I wait for you to change? You look a sight, but I daresay everyone will have heard about Barry, and they'll be frightfully impressed."

"No," he said, thinking for a moment. "I believe

I'll stay in." He needed time to think. There was a tangled feeling inside him that needed sorting out. He took his leave of Palmer and went upstairs to his rooms.

Fate. Whether you ran from it or chased it down, there was nothing you could do to escape it.

Bradley, his valet, was too used to his ways to exclaim over his battered appearance, but immediately rang for the bathwater to be brought up.

"Is there anything else you will require, my lord?" he asked. "A raw beefsteak, perhaps?"

Iverley smiled. "No, I think I will do well enough without. Though, if you could ask a man to run down to Hatchard's for me, I believe I'd like a book."

"A book?" Barrow echoed with something almost like disbelief.

"Yes," Iverley replied, somewhat perplexed himself. "I believe I should like to start reading poetry."

Twenty-three

Georgiana sat in front of the looking glass with a stubborn expression on her face. Her maid was pinning spring flowers into her hair, but she found she could not force much enthusiasm for how she looked.

Iverley would be there, of course. He could not very well miss his sister's wedding. It would have made sense, then, that she would want to look her best, but she had the obstinate inclination to show by her turn-out that she had not made any special preparations for his benefit.

No, she had spent the best part of the winter trying to get over him; she wouldn't fall back into that horrible trap of caring, just because she saw him in person. At least she wouldn't show it.

But all those memories had come back so vividly. Especially now, when they were wedding guests at the Evershams' country estate. It was impossible to see the earl and his wife without wondering what it would have been like to have been their daughter-in-law. She and Caro had walked the grounds, Caro pointing out the places where she and Vaughn had played as children. It was strange to picture him as a boy. And somehow those thoughts always led to thoughts of the children she might have had with him.

No. She jerked herself back into the present. Things were better as they'd happened. What kind of life would those children have had if their parents had not loved each other? Or rather, if they'd seen that their father despised their mother.

Her own mother bustled in with an armload of wraps. "Are you ready, my dear? The carriage will be here any moment. William has already gone to the church. Poor creature, I believe he was quite nervous."

Perhaps Iverley was already in the house. He was to have arrived up from London late last night. Georgiana's nerves felt tight from waiting for the inevitable moment when they would meet for the first time since he left Lincolnshire.

She would be calm. She would be pleasant to him. She would not let her mind be polluted with the painfully beautiful what-ifs.

Lady Eversham looked in the open doorway. "Georgiana, you look lovely. Are you nearly ready? Caro has been asking for you. She wants your opinion on the flowers she is to carry." Iverley's mother smiled affectionately. "I am so happy that my daughter will have such charming sisters-in-law. She was so very lonely in her first marriage."

Georgiana stood up. "I'll go to her, ma'am."

"Georgiana is so delighted to be a real sister to Caroline. They became so close last autumn," she heard her mother saying as she left the room. "And of course since Richard is such great friends with Vaughn, we are just like one big family."

"Vaughn speaks so well of your family," Lady Eversham agreed. "After his visit to you, he was a changed man."

Changed indeed. Georgiana hoped Lady Eversham would never know the reason for her son's bitterness.

After today the test would be over. She would go back to Lincolnshire with her mother and Emily, and she would never have to face Iverley again. If she could only make it through today.

She knocked at the door to Caro's room and then entered. Iverley's sister turned from the window. Her pale yellow dress was simple, as befitted a second wedding, but its lines flattered her slender figure and the color made her happy face appear radiant. "What do you think?" she asked, with a nervous laugh. "Will I suit?"

Georgiana ran up to her and embraced her. "You are beautiful," she said. "William will have to be revived with smelling salts. I'm so happy for you, Caro. No one deserves a doting husband more than you do, and I assure you, Will has praised you to the skies until we are all green with envy over your perfection."

Caroline took up a bouquet of flowers and smiled. "Not too ostentatious? I feel like it is wrong for me to seem too pleased over this marriage."

Georgiana looked at her in confusion.

"I was not overly happy in my marriage to Markham," she said. "And I'm afraid it will appear bad ton if I show that I am overjoyed to be marrying someone so much better suited to me this time."

Georgiana laughed. "You're a goose to worry. Everyone knows you are happy, and we are all happy because of it. And the flowers are perfect."

Caro gave her a crooked smile. "I will be a good deal more happy when this is over with. You would think that since I have done this before, I should not be so nervous, but I am. This means so much to me, Georgie."

"It was meant to be," she said, with quiet conviction. "There is no need to be nervous about something that was destined." Out the window, she saw the coach pull up to the steps. She smiled. "Your horses await. It will be done soon enough. Will is waiting for you at the church, just as nervous as you—"

The door opened and Iverley walked in. For a moment, their eyes met in silence. Georgiana was stunned, unable to move or speak. She'd expected him to be here, of course, but had he always been so handsome? Had he always been so tall? So serious-looking?

He started and cleared his throat. It was a long time before he broke the look between them and turned to his sister. "Mother said you were ready," he said shortly. "I'll take you down."

Caroline drew a breath and then turned and kissed Georgiana on the cheek. "In a few moments I'll be Mrs. Palmer," she said, her eyes sparkling. "I'll be William's wife."

Iverley was looking at her with a gaze so intense that even the simplest words failed her entirely. Georgiana felt herself blush, pale, and then go red again. He said nothing, and she remained so dumbstruck that she was forced to pretend to be looking for her gloves until he led his sister from the room.

It took three carriages to get everyone to the church, but they managed to arrive with only one disaster to Emily's gown and a panicked moment when William thought he had left the ring behind at the house. The ring was discovered in his waistcoat pocket, the clergyman began, and in a very short while, it was over.

Caroline and William went to sign the registry and Georgiana passed her handkerchief over to her mother who was enjoying a celebratory weep with Lady Eversham. She looked up to see that Iverley's eyes were again upon her. She did not know whether to smile or scowl, so she merely dropped her eyes to her lap and pretended she did not feel his continued gaze.

She'd expected him to ignore her. He was too much the gentleman to take her to task again over what had happened. But why did he continually look at her? Merely to discomfort her?

Then the new Mr. and Mrs. Palmer emerged from the vestry and there was joyous confusion and congratulations enough to cover her consternation.

The wedding breakfast was filled with so many people that it ensured that she did not have to converse with Iverley. She could have spent the whole afternoon without setting eyes on him, if she had been so fortunate as to not be tinglingly aware of wherever he stood in the room.

And it would have been easier to forget his presence, if every time she had looked up at him he hadn't been looking directly at her.

By the time the breakfast was over and the couple was sent on their way on their honeymoon, it was well into the afternoon. Lady Eversham would not hear of anyone leaving, so they rolled up the rugs and set out the card tables, and everyone prepared to enjoy themselves for the rest of the evening.

Emily bounded up to her as she stood talking to Iverley's father. "Georgie, I want to dance. Hill and Ballinghurst will, and I daresay we can get together at least nine or ten more couples. Do say you will—it will be so jolly."

"Oh, Emily, I don't really feel much like dancing," she admitted. Without Caro here, it was strange in the house. Her reason for being at Eversham Park was gone, and she felt a creeping guilt being here, talking to Iverley's parents, laughing with his friends, invading the house he had grown up in. He must be furious that she had violated the sanctity of his ancestral home.

Emily made a face of disappointment. "But if you don't, Mama will say that I can not."

"What?" boomed the earl. "Of course you shall dance. I will be your partner. Come along, my dear. We shall open the dancing together."

Georgiana watched them instruct the musicians and gather together the other young people. Iverley, across the room, smiled faintly. For a moment, she had the ridiculous notion that he was going to come and ask her to dance. But he merely looked at her for a moment, then turned and left the room.

She retreated to the card room, chastising herself for allowing her hopes to run roughshod over reality.

Her mother bustled over, looking very pleased. "I am so very glad that there are so many eligible men here," she murmured, latching herself on to Georgiana's elbow. "And a good many of them are known to you. It will not be the least bit of trouble for you to secure the interest of any number of them," she said with an arch smile. "I shall have two children married in the space of a year. And I daresay Emily will take. If she would only learn not to be such a romp."

Georgiana looked at her mother in surprise. "These are only the same old friends from home. And the new men here are just like the old. All sporting men."

Mrs. Palmer made a face of faint irritation. "You didn't used to be so particular about sporting men. Emily will be going to Town in the spring for the Season and I can't very well leave you at home. You'll perish from boredom. And your prospects of meeting an eligible man in Coningsby are very slim. Perhaps you could go to your Aunt McBee in Edinburgh. That would ensure that you wouldn't meet sporting men at any rate. I can't see that you would meet anyone at all, but we must hope."

"I am happy to stay at home at Coningsby Hall," she said calmly. "You know I'm well able to amuse myself. Besides"—she laughed—"you will want to keep at least one daughter at home to aid you in your old age."

Her mother showed a glimmer of a smile. "I don't see why I couldn't live with you and your husband. We mothers have few joys in our old age besides plaguing our sons-in-law by living with them." She sobered and looked her daughter in the face. "I know you were disappointed by Iverley," she said gently. "But you have a duty to your family."

The name still had the power to produce a painful, empty feeling inside her. How peculiar, when she had heard it so often of late. "Yes," she said in a low voice, "I know my duty." Doubtless there would come a time when she would indeed have to marry someone. But not just yet.

"Ah! Miss Palmer!" Lord Quigley called out. "You're here at last. I was hoping you'd join Pawson, Bradford, and me in a game of whist. We had such a grand time at Bell's party."

"I would love to," she replied, unable to help smiling back. It was nice to know that the friends she had gathered during her stint as a hoyden had not abandoned her. And she did rather find that she enjoyed being treated as a favorite little sister rather than some proper miss.

"Bradford is mad to tell you about the bay that he bought. I'd say it's touched in the wind, but of course he won't believe it until you tell him."

They sat down to play, but she found it very hard to keep her mind on the game.

"You're looking well this evening," Richard said, dropping into a chair beside her several rubbers later. "Meant to tell you earlier."

Georgiana's brows rose. "You must want to borrow money. You never compliment me otherwise," she said dryly. "Well you'll have to go to Mama. My luck's out tonight." A smile pulled at the corners of her mouth. "Luckily she's looking very well tonight too."

"That's unfair," said Richard, looking vaguely guilty. "You *are* looking well tonight. Much better than you have been. You've looked quite hagged of late."

He was oblivious to the jaundiced look she shot him.

"Have you been in the gardens?" he asked. He looked over her shoulder at the cards and pointed out one she should discard.

"No. I went and saw them yesterday, and it is far too cold to be jaunting about outside tonight." Somehow walking about in gardens at night tended to bring back memories it was better not to recall.

"It's nearly spring," he insisted. "Eversham has lit torches everywhere. Quite warm really. You will be sorry if you don't go."

Since when had Richard been so concerned with what she did or didn't do at a party? "Perhaps later." She looked at her hand and played the last few cards. "Ah, very well, I'm done here. I played badly tonight," she said, smiling at her partner across the table. "Do forgive me, Tony. I've caused you nothing but grief. Ask Mrs. Jonesborough to take my place and you shall trounce everyone." She excused herself and stood. "Dance with me, Richard?"

He wrinkled his nose. "I say, I'd really rather not. I just finished a set with Emily, and she stepped all over me. I don't know why Mama didn't make her wait until she gained a little grace before she let the girl go romping about." A cunning look crossed his face. "How about we go to the garden instead?"

"Why so insistent on the garden?"

He thought for a moment. "Because it's pretty," he blurted out at last.

"Since when did you care about pretty gardens? You've plotted something, haven't you? You're going to get me out there and play a trick on me or some such thing."

He looked painfully innocent. "Of course not. No tricks at all. Come on."

She reluctantly rose and sent for her wrap. "Shall I get Emily?"

"No, don't bother with her," he replied with a casual shrug that only served to convince her further that he was plotting. "Let's just go."

The spring night was cool after the closeness of the ballroom. It was warmer than the night she'd walked in the garden with Iverley, but just as clear and bright. The white light of the moon was warmed by the dancing flames of hundreds of torches in the garden below.

"See, look, statues of dancing nymphs. They've got water spurting out of their—well, hmm. Interesting, anyway. Thomlinson should get some like that." Richard led her along, his wanderings seeming suspiciously directed. "The reflecting pool," he said, as though he were surprised to come upon it. "Isn't that pretty?"

It was more than pretty. It was magical. Small candles floated on wooden bowls shaped like lily pads. Their tiny flickering lights reflected gold in the silky blackness of the pool. Torches marched along the length of the rectangle, making it appear a long, ceremonial avenue for a frightening, yet fascinating, pagan ritual.

Strains of music floated out, just like they had on the night. . . . "Let's go back. I'm cold."

"No. Wait. Not yet. I bet Emily would like to see this. I'll go get her while you wait here." He deposited her on the narrow ledge of the pool.

"Richard," she said in a warning tone. "If you've gotten some of your friends hidden around here, and they're going to leap out and scare me, I will kill you."

"No," he insisted. "No trick at all. I'll be back in two shakes."

Before she could insist that she didn't have any desire to be left here alone in this lonely, dark place, he had hurried off.

She rolled her eyes and settled down to wait. There was little point in spoiling Richard's plan, whatever it was. She half expected a band of costumed pirates to swing out of the trees, or a figure swathed in bedsheets to stagger moaning toward her. But everything was silent except for the thin high melody of the violins in the house.

She smiled and hummed along quietly, calmly waiting for the grand joke. But nothing came. She was beginning to feel a little uncomfortable. Why had Richard dragged her out here only to abandon her? It was absurd. She rose to her feet, preparing to go back to the house, when she saw a dark shape at the far end of the pool.

"Richard." She sighed in disgust. But there was no reply but a faint splash. For a moment she saw nothing, but then, how peculiar, she saw that there was a small wooden sailboat bobbing through the harbor of giant lily pads. After several collisions and nearly capsizing, it floated close enough for her to take it up. It was painted a jaunty red and white, a perfect imitation of William and Richard's *Missus*. More teasing for her mishap with the boat, she suspected. There was a piece of foolscap tucked into the little bow. She placed the boat beside her and with an indulgent smile, unrolled it. It was a verse from Byron's *Don Juan,* from the scene of his tribulations and heartbreak upon the ship leaving Spain.

> "And Oh! If e'er I should forget, I swear—
> But that's impossible, and cannot be—
> Sooner shall this blue ocean melt to air,
> Sooner shall earth resolve itself to sea,
> Than I resign thine image, oh my fair!
> Or think of anything excepting thee;
> A mind diseased no remedy can physic—
> (Here the ship gave a lurch, and he grew sea-
> sick.)"

She smiled, thinking of another man she knew who was just as averse to the sea. But the slanted black writing was neither Richard's nor William's. She looked around her in the dark. It couldn't be.

"I started with Byron," a familiar voice said quietly. "Rather less bad than I thought it would be. I tried Cowper, I truly did. But he does prose on."

Twenty-four

Georgiana leapt to her feet, the paper crumpled in her fist. Iverley could not tell by her expression if she was pleased to see him or not.

"Yes," she said unsteadily, "he does prose on." They stood staring at each other for a moment or two. "What are you doing here?" she asked at last.

"Well," he reminded her, "it is my house."

She smiled weakly, looking as though she very much wished herself on the other side of the earth. He felt suddenly awkward. He'd been mooning after her all evening and then had engineered this dramatic ploy to get her alone. He'd planned what to say, but somehow, when she looked at him, the words had scattered like birds.

The last time they'd been together, he'd said such unspeakably cruel things. How could he make her believe that he'd come to his senses? He could not, after four months' absence, just step back into her life, announce that he had been magnanimous enough to forgive her for scheming to catch him, and expected her to fall into his arms again.

He recalled with painful clarity that she had rejected his proposal of marriage. Despair twisted in his gut. What had made him think that this would not be the same?

"The wedding was lovely, wasn't it?" she asked, as though this were a normal drawing room conversation. He noticed though that her fingers continued to tighten around the ball of paper in her fist. Her face, like her fingers was growing strained.

He should have written her. He should have warned her that he had not given up. In his mind he'd needed to prepare himself, to re-create himself as someone worthy of her. But he realized now that he'd dashed out of the wings with the melodramatic flourish of a lead actor, when he was not in the least bit certain that the play was still running.

"Yes," he answered. "I am certain they'll be very happy." He scrabbled about in his head, trying to find the elaborate speech he'd planned.

This was the setting for it. This was the moment. Above him the half moon was fringed along the edge as though it had been torn. It had been so the night of Tomlinson's party. Again they had been in a garden alone. But that night she had been in love with him. He felt a knot tighten inside him.

"I'm certain Naples will be lovely this time of year. I'm so glad that is where they decided to honeymoon."

"Yes," he agreed, wishing he'd studied social graces as hard as he'd studied poetry.

"I believe it is quite warm there this time of year," she continued. "I've never been, of course. But I'm told the climate is quite pleasant."

She was even more beautiful than he remembered. Her dark hair heightened the whiteness of her skin and the pale, clear blue of her eyes. Of course, he had rarely seen her gowned for a ball. Most of their time together had been spent hunting and driving. Somehow, standing there in silk and gossamer, she seemed very feminine. A new person entirely.

She had run out of facts about Naples and stood there, twisting her fingers in her gloves as she had the night they had first met. The silence stretched longer, growing tighter like a silk thread. An expression of confusion, and perhaps hurt, crossed her face. It was replaced by resolution, and she turned to go.

"Georgiana," he called after her, "walk with me for a moment." She hesitantly took the arm he offered, and they fell in step, each pretending to admire the fountains and flowers that adorned the garden. The light weight of her hand on his arm made his nerves ache with longing.

"I wanted so much to see you," he said at last.

To his surprise, she shook her head. "Please don't, Iverley. Please don't put me through this again. I've said everything I can say. I can't apologize anymore."

He caught her hands in his own. "I don't want your apology."

She stared up at him. Her face was still, but he could see troubled shadows in her eyes. "Then what do you want?"

He felt her try to reclaim her hands and pressed them tighter. They were cold and so small, so delicate. If only he could give her the romance she deserved. Who was he, an oaf with none of the polish and grace of the poets she so admired, to make flowery declarations? "Well," he said, feeling helpless, "you."

At her stunned look, he began again. He was a plain man, and ordinary words would have to do. "I love you, Georgiana. Maybe it isn't how the poets love people, and maybe I'm not the man you made me out to be, but I do." He drew a deep breath. "I will never forgive myself for not grabbing you up when I had the chance. And if I can't forgive myself, I can't see how you would."

He felt that he was floundering. He'd never been good with words.

"But I wanted you to know that I regret my hastiness and my rudeness after you told me about . . . about your plan." God, but he was making a mull of it. A boy in calf love would have done it better. "And I love you." He smiled wanly. "Did I mention that? I love you."

She was looking at him as though he were a bed-lamite.

"Am I going to have to quote Byron to you? I will, you know. I've learned stanza upon stanza of the wretched stuff."

"Vaughn"—her smile was sad—"you love that woman I pretended to be. I'm not really her."

A curl of her dark hair had escaped its pins and lay lightly against her cheek. He took it and smoothed it back, leaving his hand against the silken warmth of her hair. "That's not true, Georgie. What I love about you is not whether you hunt or drive or spend your time playing pianoforte or sewing; what I love about you is you. I love the way your nose wrinkles up when you laugh. I love the way you tease me when I get pompous. I love your courage and your determination and your kindness."

Her forehead was drawing up in an expression of disbelief, so he took her face between his hands. "You think that I don't know you just because you pretended to like the things I like to do. But you could never hide who you really are. You couldn't hide your wit or your generous nature. I know you. And I want to know you better." He bent his head to rest his forehead against hers. "Please let me."

"It's been a long time, Vaughn," she said quietly. "We both must have changed."

He gave a rueful laugh. "I have. I've been miserable.

I've missed you. I liked myself when I was with you. I liked *us* when we were together.

"I've spent a long time thinking," he continued before she could object. "At first I was hurt, and then I thought that it would be best to give us both time apart. I didn't know what you thought of me after the way I'd treated you, the things I'd said. Caro said you were happy, so I thought . . ."

"I couldn't very well let her tell you that I was otherwise," Georgiana said with a rueful half smile. But she did not pull herself away from him.

"I didn't know," he admitted. "I didn't trust myself anymore. I convinced myself that you had fooled me. That you had made yourself up."

"I did."

"No, you didn't. You pretended to like things I enjoy doing. You didn't become a different person." He looked down into her eyes, begging her to listen to him. "You were still *you*. What was between us was still there. I regret nothing from last autumn, only that it took me so long to find the courage to come to you and admit that I was wrong to have left."

Her face was warm between his hands. He wanted nothing more than to kiss her, as he had that night in the garden, but winning back her love was more important. Her blue eyes were intently focused on his face, but she had not said she still cared. He brushed a finger against her mouth and saw it tremble.

"The time we spent together was magical," he continued. "And it doesn't matter that you took up sporting in order to spend time with me. That isn't what made it special." He took her chin to be certain that she was listening to him. "You made it special."

He saw a tentative smile pull at her lips.

"You can't resist it, Georgie. Fate and I have teamed

up to win you and there is no way you can resist us." His thumb moved against her lips. "If I ask you to marry me, are you going to try to kill me again? Drown me? Clock me over the head?"

"No, I won't try to kill you." Her voice was so low he could barely hear it.

"Then will you?"

"Marry you?" Her face in the dark was pensive.

The sound of music from the house sounded loud in the silence, but he could barely hear it through the pounding of his heart.

"On two conditions," she said at last, with a little shake in her voice.

"Anything, my love."

She looked at him with a serious expression. "Will you kiss me again, like you did that night in the garden?"

He exhaled the breath he had been holding. "Well, if that's what it takes," he said with a wry smile.

He drew her into his arms and bent his head to kiss her. She responded with such passion that he knew she had been waiting as long as he had. She was right. It was Fated. He'd fought it for too long, but it had always been meant to be.

"And the other condition?" he whispered against her lips.

She opened her eyes, and he saw that they were filled with laughter. "May we safely leave sailing off our sporting repertoire?"

Twenty-five

Iverley walked out of the tailor's establishment on Bond Street with the parcel of wedding clothes under his arm. Strange, how in one month his whole outlook on life had changed. Fate, Georgiana's voice in his head reminded him. He'd spent most of the winter struggling against its gentle grasp, and now, he couldn't wait to race headlong into it.

Georgiana had revealed something new to him every day. It was like watching a flower unfurl, each petal a new facet to her personality, her interests.

"Hello, Iverley."

He knew the calm voice perfectly before he even looked up. How ironic. Here of all places. In front of the very tailor's shop where he'd met Georgiana. When he'd been carrying another set of wedding clothes.

"Hello, Lady Hepplewell."

She extended her gloved hand, and he shook it. Muriel looked the same, and yet she was different. She was still beautiful, of course, but it did not move him. His chest did not constrict with that strange feeling of joy as it did when he saw Georgiana. "You are looking well. Down for the Season early?"

"Yes, you know I can't stand the country."

"Lord Hepplewell is in good health, I trust." He

smiled politely, feeling a bit foolish. They hadn't seen each other for a full year, and yet they were instantly reduced to the most commonplace remarks. He resisted the urge to stare. It was so strange that he had ever even considered her for his wife.

"Yes," she said, with a negligent wave of her hand. "Though he complained of rheumatics the whole winter. We might have gone to Bath, but no one goes there anymore. I hear sea bathing is quite the thing to do." She shrugged her elegant shoulders. "I don't know if it is the thing for rheumatics, but I daresay we shall have to try it."

She didn't look as though her chest had ever constricted with a feeling of joy when she thought of her husband.

"I hear," Muriel said, with an arch smile, "that you are soon to be congratulated."

"Indeed I am."

She took his arm and they walked up the street together, followed at a distance by her maid and groom. It was just like old times. Comfortable, bland, eminently proper.

"Richard Palmer's sister, am I correct? I recollect her from last Season." Muriel's pale brows drew together. "I must say, I'm surprised at your choice."

He could not help but smile. How could he ever explain something like destiny to someone like Muriel. "Why is that?" he asked mildly.

"Well, she's lovely to be sure. And certainly well bred. But she seemed to me to be a very quiet, retiring sort of girl. I know she received several offers. At least, I've heard she did. But she didn't accept any of them. Perhaps she was waiting for you." She gave him one of her rare teasing smiles.

"She was," he said. "She was waiting for me." The

pride bubbled up within him and escaped as an inane grin.

Lady Hepplewell looked entirely nonplussed. She amended her expression in time to bow at a pair of her acquaintances who were staring at them with great interest. Iverley gave them the mildest smile in return. Let them talk; the whole world knew he was in love with Georgiana.

"Yes, everyone is saying you're quite over the moon for her," Muriel said, as though her thoughts had gone in the same direction. "They say you go to the opera and to art galleries . . . I've heard you're more often found in a literary salon than in Jackson's boxing salon these days."

"I have broadened my horizons," he said, with a bow. "Wouldn't wish to be thought a rattlebrained Corinthian all my life, you know. I've come to enjoy it, actually. The opera is fairly excruciating still, but there's hope for me yet. The poetry I quite like. In fact, I was just thinking, that the use of the sea as a metaphor for—"

She looked at him as though he were an utter stranger. "Really, Vaughn, you have changed. There was a time when you never would have talked such nonsense. She's entirely bewitched you. Are you certain you have thought this through?" Her expression was serious. "Are you certain that you know her well enough?"

He stopped and looked her full in the face. "Muriel, she's perfect for me. She's everything I didn't know I wanted. I've changed because I wanted to change. I needed to change. I was in a little world, and she's broadened it." He gave a half laugh, feeling foolish and at the same time proud. "She is what I need."

Muriel was silent for a moment, the small smile tight on her face. "I see that. I see that now." She looked down, her face hidden by her bonnet. "I only wish I had been half so wise."

He felt a sudden flash of pity for his former fiancée. He remembered a conversation he'd had with Georgiana long ago. She'd wondered if there would come a day when Muriel would meet the man she was meant for and find that she could not have him. Poor Muriel. She'd played her cards for power, not for love, and now she was shackled to an old man with nothing but a title to relieve the tedium of his personality. He patted her finely gloved hand. "I'm sorry."

In a moment the expression was gone. "Goodness, what is the time?" She pulled out the delicate gold watch that was pinned to her bodice. "I'm afraid I must run. I'm to meet Sally Jersey at two and I'm a quarter of an hour late already. Of course Sally will be half an hour late, but I must run nonetheless." Her face relaxed into a genuine smile. "I'm glad we met. I wanted to congratulate you."

"Thank you." He thought for a moment. "Richard said that one day I would thank you for throwing me over. He was right, of course. We didn't suit."

"No," she said simply. "We didn't." She shook his hand and turned to go. At the last moment she looked back over her shoulder. "Tell Miss Palmer I should like to call upon her and congratulate her as well." She smiled. "She must be a remarkable woman."

Vaughn laughed aloud. "Indeed she is."

Epilogue

"How pleasant it is to see you again, Iverley," said Hennings, leaning over to shake hands over his horse's neck. "Haven't seen you since last autumn. It is excellent weather for the hunt today."

Iverley drew a breath of the cool autumn air. "Excellent weather," he affirmed. The idea that he'd ever felt a rivalry with this man was somewhat amusing.

"I hear," the man said with a smile, "that you've had a change in status since then. My congratulations. Will your wife be riding with us today?"

His wife. It still sounded strange. He'd practiced saying it every day since they married two months ago, but it still gave him pleasure to say it. "Yes. My wife will indeed be joining us."

"You know," said Hennings, "it was always you she loved. I shouldn't have proposed, knowing she felt as she did." He shrugged good-naturedly. "But I thought I'd give it a go."

Iverley smiled. "Any man in his right mind would have proposed to her," he said, with a grand gesture. "But unfortunately, I don't believe you would have been well matched."

Hennings grinned his concession. "Likely not. She's far too dashing for me."

Vaughn nodded toward a figure riding over the hill, wearing a long ostrich feather in her riding hat. "Ah," he said as though it were a great surprise, "here she is. I see she's brought her younger sister."

His friend gave a start and blushed scarlet. "I didn't know Miss Palmer was interested in fox hunting."

"Oh yes," Iverley assured him. "Emily has suddenly conceived a great interest in it."

"Hello, Lord Hennings. Hello, my love." Georgiana smiled at him. "I'm afraid the animal we'd hoped to mount Emily on proved too large. We had to saddle another so we are late."

"I'm so sorry, Lord Hennings," Emily said sweetly. "I hope we haven't delayed the drawing."

"Not at all," he stammered. "Is this your first time out, Miss Palmer? I should be glad to help you along. You know, show you how best to get along."

Emily beamed at him. "I would like that very much."

"You," said Iverley to his wife as the pair rode away, "are a very meddlesome woman."

Georgiana laughed. "And you, my husband, are a very conniving man." They turned their horses to follow the rest of the riders across the field. "Lord Hennings doesn't in the least bit seem to mind such meddling," she said. "In fact, he came to me just the other day to ask if I could recommend any music that he might bring back for Emily when he next rides in to Lincoln."

"He does seem to have an insatiable ability to listen to the harp," he conceded.

"Gone away!" shouted the huntsman as the hounds set up a long cry and set off across the countryside.

"Yes." Georgiana pretended to muse. "And he'll even sit through an entire portfolio of Mama's bird drawings. One might almost think he wished for meddling."

They followed leisurely at the back of the group of hunters, happy just to ride out and enjoy the fine day.

"Richard is furious with you for declining to meet with Hartfield," Georgiana said after they had cleared the first fence. "He said the Fancy lost its greatest gem when you stopped boxing."

Vaughn laughed. "What the Fancy lost, I gained in keeping most of my body parts intact. Hartfield is an animal. I'm sure Richard and the rest of the boxing world would have been highly amused to see me rent limb from limb, but as a respectably married man, I'm afraid I'm obliged to retain my health for higher purposes."

Her blue eyes were suddenly serious. "I would not like it if I thought you had given up something you love simply because I did not care for it."

Someone ahead of them had spotted the fox, and given a shout. Iverley reined in, allowing the rest of the field to race on ahead with the dogs.

"Georgie," he said quietly, "I did not give it up only because you did not like it. I gave it up because I no longer enjoy the idea of having my nose broken." He smiled meaningfully at her. "Different things are important to me now."

He enjoyed seeing her blush slightly. "I feel the same," she said with great gravity. "I've entirely given up playing the pianoforte, for instance."

"You hated playing," he reminded her.

Their horses took them up the hill toward the line of trees that ringed the estate. He realized with a smile that it was the same woods in which he had been thrown from his horse that autumn day so long ago. He was strangely sentimental about the place.

She made a pretty moue. "Yes. But I was told that it was a necessary skill in the pursuit of a husband."

"Obviously a fallacy."

"Indeed, I was misinformed. I should have studied *Weekly Dispatch* instead of French and practiced my left hook instead of needlework."

The hunters were now so far ahead of them that they could barely hear the cries of the dogs. He slowed his horse to a walk. "Those skills would have caught you nothing but a rattle of a Corinthian who used his brains for nothing more than to endanger them."

"Yes," she said thoughtfully. "Fortunately, instead I married an extremely well-read man whose intellect is as keen as his other skills.

"Though you will continue to buy hunters who are a good deal too highly strung under the delusion that they are spirited." She continued in a teasing tone, though there was a softness to her expression.

He reined in his horse. The sound of the dogs was distant now. They were entirely alone. "I believe my animal should be walked for a while. A horse so highly strung is likely to throw me as he did in this same woods last year."

He dismounted and then went to help Georgie down from her horse. His hands remained at her waist even once she stood on the ground.

She smiled up at him. "Was it only a year?"

"Does it seem like longer or shorter?"

She thought for a moment, perfectly content to remain in the circle of his arms. "Both," she said at last. "Longer because much of the time I was miserable and convinced that I should never see you again. And shorter"—she leaned her forehead against his shoulder—"shorter because I now have the rest of my life to spend with you."

She pulled back from him and put her arms around his neck. "I knew from the start that you were perfect for me, Vaughn," she said in a low voice. "I know I shouldn't have gone about things how I did, but I knew, I just knew, that we should be together."

He looked down into his wife's smiling face. "And who am I, my love," he said, leaning in to kiss her, "to resist Fate?"

ABOUT THE AUTHOR

CATHERINE BLAIR lives in New York. She is currently working on her next Zebra Regency romance, *A Scholarly Gentleman,* which will be published in August 2002. Catherine loves to hear from readers and you may write to her c/o Zebra Books. Please include a self-addressed stamped envelope if you wish a response.

BOOK YOUR PLACE ON OUR WEBSITE AND MAKE THE READING CONNECTION!

We've created a customized website just for our very special readers, where you can get the inside scoop on everything that's going on with Zebra, Pinnacle and Kensington books.

When you come online, you'll have the exciting opportunity to:

- View covers of upcoming books
- Read sample chapters
- Learn about our future publishing schedule (listed by publication month *and author*)
- Find out when your favorite authors will be visiting a city near you
- Search for and order backlist books from our online catalog
- Check out author bios and background information
- Send e-mail to your favorite authors
- Meet the Kensington staff online
- Join us in weekly chats with authors, readers and other guests
- Get writing guidelines
- AND MUCH MORE!

Visit our website at
http://www.kensingtonbooks.com

More Zebra Regency Romances

Discover The Magic of
Romance With

Jo Goodman